"You damn near got me killed," Beck says, dropping his fingers to the fabric of the boxers and then sliding them down until he touches the bare skin of my inner thighs. I moan and arc my hips, naturally moving towards him and the growing bulge in his pants. The lust I feel for this man is like an unstoppable force. It's scaring the crap out of me, to be honest. But what am I going to do? I've never felt anything like this in my whole life, and I don't know how to fight it. "Damn near got me killed," he repeats, unzipping his pants and freeing his cock. It springs forward like it's got a mind of its own, straining for me, desperate to be inside. I close my eyes so tight they hurt and then open them again, finding Beck's dark gaze in the moonlight. His face is covered in shadow, carving out spots where his cheekbones are, his eyes, his lips. It's a little eerie, but in a sexy, mysterious sort of way.

BOOKS BY C.M. STUNICH

The Seven Wicked Series

First
Second
Third
Fourth
Fifth
Sixth
Seventh

Houses Novels

The House of Gray and Graves
The House of Hands and Hearts and Hair
The House of Sticks and Bones

The Huntswomen Trilogy

The Feed
The Hunt
The Throne

Indigo Lewis Novels

Indigo & Iris
Indigo & The Colonel
Indigo & Lynx

Never Say Never Trilogy & Never Too Late Series

Tasting Never
Finding Never
Keeping Never
Never Can Tell

Triple M Series

Losing Me, Finding You
Loving Me, Trusting You
Needing Me, Wanting You
Craving Me, Desiring You

A Duet

Paint Me Beautiful
Color Me Pretty

Needing Me, Wanting You

C.M. STUNICH

SARIAN ROYAL

ISBN-10: 1938623738 (pbk.)
ISBN-13: 978-1-938623-73-8 (pbk.)

"Triple M" Name Used With Permission From
Melissa, Mireya, and Megan of "Triple M Bookclub"
Optimus Princeps font © Manfred Klein
Ink In the Meat Font © Billy Argel
Jenna Sue Font © Cheap Pro Fonts
Stock images © Shutterstock.com
Cover art and design © Amanda Carroll and Sarian Royal

this book is dedicated to the following people in no particular order. because they're incredible. because they deserve it. and mostly just because I felt like it. ;)

to Stella and Lee from Boston
to Rachael Rushing Pennington
to Amy Jerome
to Susan Harris Avila
to Tracie Blankenship

and of course, to all the wonderful bloggers, readers, and friends I've met along the way. just because your name isn't on this list, doesn't mean I don't heart you.

much love.

Tease
CHAPTER 1

I like my job because it's easy. The most difficult part of my day consists of choosing what color eyeshadow to wear, which corset makes me look the curviest. I'm not saying that what I do is going to change the world, but it's all I know, so I roll with it. I think my dad was disappointed in me though. I don't know why, but I always got that feeling when his eyes meet mine from across the room. *Like father, like daughter, Dad,* I think as I move across the carpet in my heels. Unfortunately, he's not around to ask. Not that he would've admitted it anyway. My dad and I had a strange relationship.

"Emilie," my brother says, greeting me with a frown and a chaste kiss. Nobody calls me that anymore, but him. Even though I can tell some serious business is brewing, I give him a smile.

"It's good to see you, bro," I say, and I get the teensiest, tiniest smile back. It only lasts so long though before it's wiped away with responsibility and worry. My brother never stops worrying. It's like a hobby for him. I shrug my jacket up my shoulders and move to the side, giving the Sergeant At Arms of our club, room to face the green-eyed devil everybody calls Tax, but who I still call Dare-Bear. Only when he's not listening, of course.

The two men stand facing each other for a moment before reaching out and shaking hands, hard and gruff. Formal. My brother is really into formalities. And he enforces them. I guess if you can keep a group of seventy-seven wild men in line with a single word, you have the right to. Since the moment our father died, Darren Jr. has been whooping ass and taking names, fighting his way to the top, doing everything in his power to preserve my father's legacies. So whether I agree with the way we do things in Seventy-Seven Brothers or not, I obey.

I look down at the floor beneath my feet, the dark carpeting of the clubhouse framing my black heels in burgundy with cream colored diamonds. I don't have any business here, but I had to see my brother. He's the one that raised me anyhow, so I owe him the courtesy. Besides, it's expected of me. I'm the only woman here who isn't an old lady. I ride with the club out of respect to who my father was, and who my brother is. To everyone else, I'm just a bitch in the garage.

It might bother some ladies, but it doesn't bother me. Despite what you might think, this isn't a blood in, blood out sort of a scenario. I'm free to walk away at any time. I just choose not to. Like I said, my job is easy, and I don't know anything else. The club is my life.

"Go get yourself something to eat, Tease," Darren tells me, nodding his chin and dismissing me, just like that. I smile again and wink at him, sliding past Oren and his vicious grin. He is absolutely relentless, even in front of my brother. Out of the entire group, that man is by far my least favorite. "I'll come see you later."

"Is that a promise?" I ask, but Darren's green eyes have already switched off, taken him out of this world and into himself. It means he's thinking about club business and not about me. It used to bother me, but it doesn't anymore. It's amazing how accustomed you can get to something you used to despise. The human race is remarkably adaptable.

A couple of the guys escort me out of the room and down the stairs. Darren might be my brother, but he's still the President of our motorcycle club. Nobody gets in there without some serious trust and a particularly thorough pat down.

Eyes follow me as I move through the halls toward the dining room. Eyes are always following me. That's sort of my whole purpose here. I'm like a walking, talking canvas, a piece of art to be admired. But never touched. A sex symbol who doesn't have sex. Does the name make sense now? Tease is not a monicker I'd have picked out for myself. But then, Emilie Hathorne doesn't work either. I guess I'm just trapped in the in-between. That's okay, though, because I've been here forever and forever I will stay.

"Hungry, princess?" one of the prospects jokes when I move into the dining room, emerging into a frenzied raucous of cheerful shouts and the clinking of silverware. The majority of the club is here tonight for our monthly get-together, and the feeling of family is almost palpable in the air. A real smile tweaks my face then as I gaze around at the crowd in leather and blue. The words *Seventy-Seven Brothers* stand out at me on the backs of jackets accompanied by two sevens outlined in white.

"The name's Tease," I tell the man, looking him up and down, immediately casting him aside as any sort of romantic interest. If he's in the MC, I'm not interested. One day, I'm afraid I'll be forced to choose someone to stay, and my chest gets tight. For now, I'm only eighteen years old, and my brother still takes care of me. I have no idea what'll happen later, when I get a little older and he stops looking at me like his little sister and more like a woman with nobody and nothing. I try to tell myself I'm being paranoid, but what happens if Darren isn't the President? What then? "And if Tax hears you calling me that, he'll beat your ass down."

I flip my hair over my shoulder and move into the room. I'm comfortable here, surrounded by all these people. A good portion of them have been around my entire life, friends to my father and now to my brother. This here is fuckin' family. I tuck my hands in my pockets for a moment and try to decide where to sit. I avoid anybody that doesn't already have an old lady by their side. I'm absolutely, one hundred percent not interested in anyone here, and I don't like people getting ideas. Ideas breed trouble when they're cast in the wrong vein. Besides, most of the men here are twice my age and while I love and respect and even admire many of them, when I do look for a partner, I'd like them to be at least close my own age.

I wander slowly through the group, listening in on snippets of conversation. I try to collect as much information as possible, just in case. You never know when it might come in handy.

"Triple M?" I hear one of my friends ask, leaning forward. Her elbows rest on the table as she runs her tongue over her lips and stares her husband, Cape, down. He's gossiping again which my brother really hates, but situated here around the dinner table, it's hard not to talk about your day. It happens sometimes. "Why does the name sound familiar?" she asks, letting her eyes roll to the ceiling in thought. "They from Virginia?"

"They're not from anywhere," Cape says, staring into his drink. I think he's had a little too much personally, but I sit down on the bench next to Angelina anyway and watch as his red face scrunches up. "They travel around the country … " Cape's voice trails off and he leans in conspiratorially, even when his brother slams his beer down onto the wooden tabletop a bit harder than necessary. "Robbing banks. Banks is their territory." Cape takes another swig of his drink and sighs. "Robbin' banks and changin' lives, I guess. They're ready to revolutionize the world, one city at a time.

Stupid motherfuckers."

"Goddamn it, Cape," Tim growls, giving his brother a dark-eyed glare. I pretend not to be interested, reaching into the basket in the center of the table and withdrawing a roll. As Tim continues, voice heavy with anger, I slather butter across the bread and put it to my lips. In a moment or two, somebody will bring me a plate; they always do. If I was here as an old lady, I'd get up and get it myself, take my husband his first. Instead, I get to sit here and pretend I'm one of the guys. It's an illusion, but I'm going to enjoy it while it lasts. "Stop running your mouth and at least get the fucking facts straight." Tim slaps one big hand into the other for emphasis. "Triple M is a joke. They rob banks and they play games. I don't know what they're getting at here, but starting shit with Bested by Crows and Broken Dallas wasn't the smartest fucking decision. If they keep at this crap, somebody's going to put them down just to prove a point."

"And what's that point?" I ask. Angelina gives me a look, adjusting the red bandanna she wears on her head. It's not just for looks: Angelina lost her hair in chemo. I reach out and curl my fingers around hers. She's my sister, and I'd do anything for her. I know she'd do the same for me. That's a good feeling. My real sister, Lizzie, she wouldn't give me the scraps from her table.

"The point is that you can't just change the way things are. That's not how the world works. There are rules and you follow 'em. If you're going to try to break boundaries and knock down walls, you have to own them. And they don't. Triple M is a bunch of wannabe riders in easy-to-order jackets. I think we should greet 'em on their way to the coast and take their cuts. They're not worthy of wearing them." Tim finishes his beer with a huff and stands up, cursing his way across the room and towards the doors in the back corner. He's probably off to smoke and play pool. That's pretty much the favorite activity around here on our Friday night get-togethers. I don't often play, mostly because nobody wants me to, but when I do, I kick all their asses.

I smile.

"Something on your mind, Tease?" Angelina asks me, and I shake my head, resting my chin in my palm. There's something comforting about being here, about knowing that every single fucking person in that room would take a bullet for you. A sense of camaraderie that's hard to find elsewhere. At the same time, it feels like there's a glass ceiling, too. Nobody talks about, but it's there. I can excel, but only in certain areas, only in the places where I'm supposed to excel. There's something soothing about that, too, believe it or not. As long as my head is hitting that ceiling, I know I'm exactly where I'm supposed to be.

I touch a hand to my stomach and think about Triple M. I've heard Oren talking about them before. *Bank robbers.*

I move my hand up my belly and rest it on my chest. My heart is pumping fast, too fast maybe. As I let my thoughts wander, it starts to speed up. Not just bank robbers.

Women with patches, with responsibilities, with bikes. *With balls.*

My soft smile turns into a grin. A big one. Spreading across my face like a sunburn.

Angelina gives me another look, like she has no idea who I am in that moment. By the time a prospect arrives with my plate, the look is gone and I'm back to blending in with the background. Where I belong. Where I'll always belong.

CHAPTER 2

Well, shoot.

I run my fingers through my hair and give the little blonde at the bar one, last grin. But she ain't buyin' my shit. Doesn't happen often, but occasionally the ladies get a whiff of my special Beck bullshit and there they go a runnin'.

"No, no, thank you. I'm fine," she says, grabbing her purse and rising to her feet. She tries to smile at me, but I can tell from the look in her eyes that she knows I'm trouble. "I don't need another drink." She gives me a look that says she ain't a fan of either my cut or my ink, maybe both. "Have a nice day." I take a sip of my beer and keep my eyes on her ass as she scurries the fuck out of the bar like she's on fire.

"Aw, baby. I could've set you aflame for real. It woulda been like fireworks in July." I finish my drink and slide it across the counter. Two seats down, Melissa Diamond is staring at me like I'm a crazy motherfucker. And I am. Honest to God, I really, truly am.

"Boo hoo," she murmurs, pouting her lips and curling her fingers around her glass. "She was real cute. A genuine Southern belle, like our Little Miss Amy Cross." Melissa bites off her words and sucks the red straw into her mouth. I give her a look that says I'm doin' my best to find our entertainment for the night, but in this town, it hasn't been easy. These beach babes are smarter than I give 'em credit for.

"Hey, baby. I'm doin' all the heavy lifting over here." I move over to her and push some hair back from her face. We have a weird relationship, the ex Mrs. Diamond and me. A friendship that nobody else understands. If she wasn't still in love with the late Mr. Diamond, we might've had a chance. But I think Melissa will always care for that scum bag sack o' shit. See, that's the thing about the L-word. You can't control it, can't decide when it bites you in the ass. I've managed to escape it so far, and here's to hopin'. Austin's been walking around with this goofy as shit grin on his damn face, and Gaine ... shoot. Fucker went about wooing his woman all the wrong way, but now? He's got that same stupid ass expression. Like they both have been shot in the foot, but are hopped up on morphine. They're both nursin' bleeding wounds they don't even know they have. How stupid is that?

"Well, try harder," Melissa soothes, spinning around on the stool with her drink. It's somethin' fancy, somethin' blue. I lean over and grab a sip through her straw.

"That's just plain fucking nasty," I tell her, touching her chin and taking a step back, letting my eyes roam around the semi-darkness of the bar. It's only been three days since we smashed the shit of out Bested by Crows. I'm no fool; shit could go wrong at any minute. I let go of Melissa and run my hands along the denim of my jeans to take note of the weapons there. *A small hammer and two knives.* I don't carry a whole lot 'cause shit, let's be honest: Beck Evans ain't a bitch. I can kill a man with my bare hands. If you know what you're doing, it isn't all that difficult either. "Why don't you have a beer like a normal person?"

"Why don't you spend less time flapping your lips and more time flirting?" Melissa says, finishing her drink and setting it on the bar behind her. "Preferably with girls that won't flip out when you suggest a threesome to them." I laugh and rub the stubble on my chin. *Damn.* The last girl we picked up together, Crystal, she was crazier than a sprayed roach. But hot.

And now she's probably six feet under and rotting.

I blink my eyes, real slow like, just to make sure nobody knows what I'm thinking about. Especially Gaine and Mireya. Last thing I'd need is to let those two assholes know how worried I really am. Far as they know, I'm a big, stupid motherfucker with loose lips and even looser morals. And yeah, I might be big, and I'm sure as shit stupid, but I know what's what. Our existence as an MC is up in the air right now. It shouldn't be, but it is.

Crazy ass Kent. We had a good thing going here. Motorcycles, madness, money. Triple M. Why'd you have to go and screw this crap up?

I glance back at Melissa. Her eyes are all faraway and cloudy again. I hate that look. Tells me she's reminiscing again. I reach out and clamp her shoulder firmly, drawing her back to the here and now. I am straight up proud of this woman. I think Gaine thinks we're in love, but that isn't it at all. I mean, I love the lady, but I'm pretty damn sure I'm not *in* love with her. I sure as shit ain't walking around with a goofy ass grin on my face. I'm just proud of her for doing what she did before, for taking her vengeance on those flaccid dick holes in Bested by Crows. Granted, it isn't entirely their fault that Kent did what he did, went rogue and all. But if Melissa hadn't been there, Gaine might not have made it out alive.

"Hey there, sugar cakes. You alright?" Melissa shrugs and gives me a sultry smile, not half as hot as it was when Kent was alive. Sometimes I think she only liked fuckin' me so much because she knew Kent would flip the fuck out if he knew. I'm not a forbidden fruit no more. *Well, crap, shit and damn it.* "You want to dance or somethin'? Go down to the beach?" We're right on the coast, and yet, I haven't touched my feet to the sand. Have barely even looked at the sparkling blue waters.

"I liked St. Marlin's better," Melissa says, looking around the room like this here bar represents the city as a whole. The dark walls and the ratty posters clinging to life with yellowed edges hardly show off what Korbin has to offer. I've been here before, and I know there is a mean ass taffy shop on the boardwalk. "I liked it the first time. Even better the second time. Why did Bested by Crows have to fuck that shit up?" Melissa doesn't answer my questions, just stands up and throws me a wink before heading towards the doors.

I don't follow after her. She wouldn't want me to anyway. The person she's waiting for is never coming back again. I can imagine how that feels. Actually, I don't even need to imagine it. I've been there, done that. And thank you, ma'am, but I am through with that shit.

I snort and run my hand through my hair. The only women left in this bar are hardened and probably immune to my special brand of charm. Best I take my search elsewhere.

I turn on my heel and push my way through the heavy green door at the front. Sunshine slams into my skin with an angry vengeance, teasing the black ink on my arms, making me squint my eyes as I scan the street around me. This here's another quiet, little Southern town with charm and a questionable affiliation with the motorcycle club, Seventy-seven Brothers. I've been worried about them for awhile now. Kimmi, too. Most MCs ride around with chapters, areas, or countries on their bottom rocker. Seventy-seven Brothers rides around with this little gem plastered on the bottom of their leather: *Should the Need Arise*. Now what the fuck does that mean?

"Jesus Lord help us all," I mutter as I pull out a cigarette and light up, smoking and winking at a pair of brunettes moving down the sidewalk opposite me. One of them tosses a light wave my way, but I stay put. I'm sure there'll be plenty more at the beach. I'm going to force myself to try and relax. There are clubs all over the States, so there's no point in running. Running won't do us a damn bit of good. If we keep doing what we do, we'll always be in somebody's territory. But it's worth the risk. Triple M is a home for those who don't fit anywhere else, who are too broken to be regular, and too regular to be broken.

"Thank God!" My lips quirk up into a smile as I take another drag and then drop the cigarette to the cement, scraping it out with my boot. "Beck, please tell me you're free for the afternoon."

"Shit, sugar. You just can't stand the thought of me gettin' laid when your bed's as dry as the damn desert." I turn to Kimmi and let my smile morph into a grin. She looks hot as usual, an untouchable bundle of rounded curves and orange hair, diamond earrings and too tight pants. I love this bitch.

She stops on a dime, plants one hand on her hip and glares daggers at me.

"Hey, if you don't want the company, let me know now and I'll get out of your hair."

I laugh and toss an arm around her neck, drawing her along beside me as we start down the sidewalk towards the beach. I can hear the sound of waves from here, a gentle lapping that belies the turmoil in our own lives. *Ah, how I miss the good ol' days.* I would have gladly ran weed for Kent forever if it meant we could keep on keepin' on. Oh well. No point in crying over spilled milk.

"You know I would never turn down a chance to scope out your tits, Reynolds," I tell her as she rolls her eyes and casts her green eyes over to mine. We have the exact same shade to our irises: green with a sliver o' shit. Kimmi and I both know how to bullshit the ladies. We used to have competitions to see who could bang more babes, but I think we've both lost count.

"Keep wishing and wanting, Evans," Kimmi says, shimmying her shoulders and sending her massive melon tits a swinging. "You will never get a chance to taste these babies."

"If I don't get a taste, why'd you come running over here? What the hell do you want now? You're not trying to skim any ladies off me, are you?" Kimmi looks around and then turns her gaze up to me, narrowing her eyes with a smile.

"I don't see any women for miles, Beck. They must've gotten a whiff of your crap and taken off running. Actually, I'm here with a very specific question in mind."

I nod my head knowingly and try to appreciate the architecture around me. Narrow roads, wide sidewalks, buildings older than my grandpa's pa. Korbin's a colorful town, too. I don't see a single building painted gray or brown or beige. There's a brick house with white trim across the street from a yellow convenience store, parking lot complete with palm trees. And over there is our hotel, pale blue with red shudders. It's a pretty little place. I push back my trepidation and keep smiling.

"This about that girl, Christy?" I ask Kimmi. She's easier to read than a damn picture book. She's been crushing on Amy's friend since the moment I picked the girl up and tossed her on my bike. "Because you know that shit's only headed two ways: down the shitter or down Austin's well traveled road of love blindness. I can't see you in either place, babe."

"Remember Cilantro?" Kimmi asks me, and my smile gets less silly, more serious. The girl Kimmi's missing is named after an herb, sure, but the fact that she pretends to forget her name? Not a good sign. She still misses that stupid bitch. The girl was so dumb she couldn't pour piss out of a boot with the instructions written on the heel. You'd have to be that friggin' stupid to walk away from a woman as wonderful as Kimmi.

"Her name was Mint, Kimmi. You know that. And of course I remember her." I grab a surreptitious look at her face. It's frozen into a neutral expression, eyes panning the horizon with disinterest. We're here in this perfect, little town and yet neither of us can find the time to relax. What a pair we make. "And it's okay if you miss her. It's okay if you miss Margot."

"I don't miss either of those bitches," Kimmi says, but I can tell she does and that's okay. I respect secrets. I got to. I got so damn many of my own. "I'm just trying to use Mint as a reference. I *felt* her, Beck." Kimmi frowns a bit, her red lips drawing down her face as she turns to look at me again. "Have you ever felt someone, Beck?"

I don't hesitate before I shake my head.

"Nope."

"In all six senses: sight, sound, taste, scent, touch." Kimmi swallows. "And ... that mysterious *everything* that you just can't quantify."

"Right." I remember this story. I've heard it a dozen times before. All it does is piss me the fuck off. *Mint, you stupid bitch. How dare you break my friend's heart? I hope you rot in the fiery depths o' hell.* I start on another cigarette, just to keep my anger in check. "So what's this got to do with Christy?"

"I don't know her. I mean, of course I don't. And she'll hardly speak two words to me, but I ... I feel like I ... like I can *feel* her. Does that make any sense?" Don't make no fucking sense to me, but I nod anyway, just to make Kimmi feel better. "Do you think she's gay? Because, I mean, I don't want to go after her if there's no hope of anything."

"You're stupid as Austin Sparks, Kimmi. Dumb as a doornail. Shoot, everybody calls me the birdbrained one, but I ain't near half as dim-witted as the two of you. Why do you want to get mixed up with a virginal little belle? That there's just asking for trouble." Kimmi kicks me in the shin with her heel as we stumble past a shop window filled with nothing but candles. Who the hell would even walk into a place like that? What's the damn point?

I remove my arm from around Kimmi's neck and grin again.

"But yeah, I think she's got rainbows shooting out of her ass."

"And why's that?" Kimmi asks me suspiciously. Nobody here believes the Beck Evans test for sexuality but me. "Wait, wait. Lemme guess. You hit on her and she said no?" I shrug and toss my cigarette into an ashtray as we pass by.

"Maybe."

"So maybe I think you're full of shit. Thank you very much." I just laugh and pause at the next intersection, looking either way for traffic. Dead and quiet. Just the way I like it. Good thing about hogs is you can hear 'em a mile away. So I keep my ears open and my eyes on the ocean. Already I'm starting to sweat, so I slide off my vest and reach my fingers under my shirt. I'd take off my jeans, too, if I wouldn't get arrested. Y'all know Beck Evans never wears underwear.

"Ugh," Kimmi says as the fabric comes up and over my head. "Are you stripping already? Can't you wait until I'm far enough away that I don't have to smell your sweaty pits?" I move closer to Kimmi and laugh as she cringes away from my baby butt smoothness. Yeah, that Crystal girl shaved me up real good. From head to toe. It's fucking weird, won't lie about that. But some girls like it, so I'm going to play off this male model shit.

"Listen babe, Christy's gay as a 1970's bathhouse. But

she's also a closeted little mouse. You've gotta approach with cheese before you can pet. Catch my drift?"

"Nobody ever catches your drift, Beck," Kimmi says, stepping off the curb and moving across the shimmering pavement. Isn't that funny how that happens? How the sunshine can make something as dead as cement look alive? I follow after my friend and pause at the brick retaining wall that separates the sidewalk from the sand. As far as the eye can see, blue stretches out, smiling at us with foamy waves and curling fingers, beckoning us into the depths. I pause and sit down to take off my boots. When I do things, I like to do them right.

"You goin' down to the surf in five inch heels and a corset, hooker?" I ask Kimmi, and she punches me in the shoulder, pausing to put her hands on her hips and scope out the beach.

"You know me. I always come prepared. I've got a G-string on under this baby." Kimmi touches her tits and pats them reverently. "But I keep the heels on. There's no debating that."

I toss my boots across the wall and step over, holding my hand out for Kimmi. She takes it and joins me with more grace in her pinky than I have in my whole damn body. I get these weird thoughts that maybe she was a gymnast before joining the club, but I've never asked. A lot of us don't. We're all here for a reason, and we got shit to hide. Look at me, a failed career in the military. A pair of hands drenched in the blood of God only knows how many. The devil's got his hand wrapped around my heart and ain't nobody wants to look at that crap.

I drop my shirt and jacket on the pile and leave it there. Nobody's going to touch that shit. And if they do? Well, God help 'em.

I lean against a palm tree and light up one more cig before I hit the surf, scanning the people milling around in the sand. Straight ahead, underneath an umbrella that they got from God knows where, sit Triple M's newest married couple: Gaine and Mireya. Seeing them together makes me feel like a huge weight's been lifted off my shoulders. I swear to Christ, if I had to spend one more Goddamn day watching Austin play with Mireya, watching Gaine stare at her from the shadows, I mighta just shot myself in the damn head.

"Feels like spring is in the air, huh?" Kimmi asks me, stripping her clothes off and not giving two fucks if anybody's looking at her in a bathing suit that's illegal in a handful of countries. My lip twitches into a smile again. I spend most of my day smilin'. I spent a lot of my younger years with a frown, so you know, I gotta make up for it.

"Triple M's like a matchmaking service, ain't it? Sign up to ride with us and get yourself a gen-u-ine soulmate for the ages." I blow out a mouthful of smoke and glance up at the sky. It's clear today, absolutely cloudless and perfect. I roll my shoulders to try and loosen up some of the tension. It's the first thing women notice. A man who's relaxed has got his shit together. A guy with tight shoulders is bad news.

It's one of them hidden facts of life that nobody tells you about.

"I think it's cute," Kimmi says, strutting up beside me in her bathing suit, nothing but a sarong around her hips. Despite her words, she's switched into a pair of sandals she got out of her purse. So much for heels on the beach. I laugh at her and push myself away from the tree, moving across the warm beach in my jeans. As I bend down to roll up the legs, I take stock of the available ladies lounging around me. There aren't many, not even on a day like this. Most of the girls I see are hanging out in groups. It's not impossible to snag their attention, but it makes it that much more difficult. Today, Beck Evans is lookin' for easy.

"Didn't think you liked the beach?" Austin asks, coming up from behind us and helping Amy over the wall. Her brunette hair is twisted up on her head and her face is practically glowing. I don't know much about the girl, but I see the way she and Austin look at each other. Two of my friends are down and out for the count. Now all I gotta do is worry about Kimmi and then I can retire a happy man.

"I made an exception today," I tell him, trying my best not to scope out his new lady. Hey, I'm warm-blooded. It's just natural, baby. "Scopin' me out some bunnies, so I don't feel so lonely no more." I give Amy a faux frown and she giggles, touching her fingers to her lips.

"You'll be hard-pressed to find any rabbits here, Mr. Evans. Possums maybe, or racoons. Perhaps a gull or two?" Amy points her finger up at the sky as Austin chuckles, weaving his fingers through hers. She blushes briefly and turns away with a sly smile on her face. Me, I just laugh because really, the whole world's funny if you look at it sideways. Best way to live. Trust me. I done gone and tried the other ways, and it left me a bitter, bitter man. Sometimes, ignorance really is bliss.

"I'll keep that in mind, Miss Cross," I drawl, reaching out and pressing a peck to her cheek. She shrieks and Austin gives me a curled lip that makes me laugh just that much harder as I turn away and start my walk down to the shore. If I don't start my search now, I could be going to dinner alone tonight. And Beck Evans never misses out on a meal.

Tease
CHAPTER 3

My brother finds me later that night, sitting on the porch smoking a cigarette and nursing a beer. My legs are curled up on the chair and in my hand is a crumpled magazine that I was only half-reading. Most of my attention is focused out on the street, at the people walking by, the cars, the sounds and smells of the city. People-watching is one of my favorite activities in life. I could sit here all day and observe, letting my mind wander into the lives of strangers. *That girl there, in the white pants and the sparkling shirt. She's got on tall heels, but no makeup. Her eyes are red like she's been crying.* I start to spin a story in my head, imagining her climbing out of bed and getting dressed for the day, putting on a nice outfit, doing her hair. Maybe she was going out to lunch with her fiancé? Maybe, as she was standing in the bathroom getting ready to put on her lipstick, she got a call. He had to cancel. He was sorry, but he didn't see their relationship going anywhere.

Shivers travel up my arms as I run my fingers over the delicate rose tattoo on my bicep. Watching people like this is akin to living a hundred lives, a thousand. I get to delve into a whole host of scenarios I'd never otherwise get the chance to participate in. I've gotten so good at it that my imagination is enough to give me an adrenaline rush.

"Did you enjoy dinner?" Darren asks, lighting up a cigarette and pretending that neither of us is bothered by the lack of privacy in our conversation. My brother doesn't go anywhere without an entourage now. The quiet nights we used to share, when I was six and he was twenty-one, sitting on his knee and reading stories about faraway places ... those are gone forever. I look up at him with a smile on my face, shifting slightly, my leather pants squeaking against the rough wood of the rocking chair. It might sit at the clubhouse now, but this used to belong to my mother. It's one of the few things of hers I brought over here. And I don't even like the reason I did. *I'm sorry, Lizzie. You pushed me to the edge, and I did petty things. If I could take them back, I would. But you, you'd never say you were sorry, would you?*

"It was wonderful, thank you," I tell him, looking up and watching the bright yellow of the porch light highlight his cheeks, the cleft in his jaw. Darren's green eyes shimmer as he takes in the scenery around the clubhouse, appreciating it but still watching. Always watching. Sometimes I think my brother is too paranoid. Nine times out of ten, whatever situation he encounters is solved without violence. Then again, maybe he's earned that blessing by being so cautious. I look away and focus my attention on a man in a suit and sneakers. Strange combo. I smile. Wonder what his story is? "The new guy, the one with a lady's name. He's real good. Best chicken and dumplings I've ever had."

"Marcy?" my brother asks as I take a drag on my cigarette. But he doesn't smile back. I've known him long enough that I can tell that something's wrong. I don't bother to ask though. He won't talk about it with me. That's club business there. I can hazard a guess though. *Triple M.* If they're anywhere near here, my brother will want to pay them a visit. We can't be perceived as weak, and allowing a group to travel through our turf, to rob us, to disrespect us, that would be a big mistake on Darren's part. He knows it; we all know it. "Weird name, good guy, excellent fucking cook."

I twist fully around in my seat, letting the magazine fall to my lap and wrapping my arms around my legs. Moths flutter gently in the air around us, green and white blurs that sparkle at the edges of my vision like stars.

"But you didn't come out here just to talk chicken and dumplings, did you, Tax?" I ask, using his nickname for the benefit of the guys. I'd much rather be calling him Dare-Bear, throwing myself into his arms and letting him hold me tight. I'm not a little girl anymore though, and that scares me. Really, really scares me. Little girls get decisions made for them; women have to make their own choices. *What if*

I'm not ready to make my own choices though? "What's up?"

I swallow hard and keep a neutral expression on my face as Tax moves forward and sits down on the patio step, nursing his beer and staring blankly outwards. My heart is fluttering in my chest, mimicking the flapping of the moths' wings. This, this could be the conversation I've been dreading for awhile now. *You're nothing but an ornament, an accessory, a hanger-on. You're like a puppy purchased at Christmas, novel at first but useless when you become a bitch.* I blink Lizzie's words away and let my eyes trace the patches on the back of Tax's jacket.

"I'm sure you've heard the rumors, right?" Tax asks, leaning his elbows on his knees. His shaggy hair looks like rubies in the waning light of the evening. I've got the same hair – everyone in my family does. Lizzie, Darren, my mom, my dad, me. It's wavy, but it behaves well. I waver between loving it and hating it. Half the time I feel like the dark red against my pale skin is beautiful, a perfect contrast. The other half of the time, I feel like it looks like blood. Old blood. Spilled and spoilt. I shake my head and brush the stray strands of hair back.

"Triple M?" I ask because it's pointless to pretend I don't know what Darren's talking about. After the tidbits I gathered in the dining room today, I can see where this is going. My heart doesn't stop beating. Yes, I'm relieved that my brother isn't here to demand that I get my shit together, but whenever I hear that name, I get light-headed and tight in the chest. *Triple M.* The crazy bikers who don't follow the rules, who don't even try to play it straight. I find myself running my tongue over my lips. I'm part of an MC, one that knows how to hold itself together, to stand strong, to fight hard. Why am I sitting here fantasizing over some outlaw group with no sense? I put the butt of my hand against my forehead, leaning forward and trying my best to catch my breath.

I don't know why I'm getting so worked up over this. I'm just doing what I always do, letting myself slip into someone else's shoes. I keep having this recurring dream where I'm soaring, dark wings spread out on either side of me as my shadow passes over mountains, fields, beaches. When I come to rest, it's on the arm of a tree that stretches so high into the sky that it pierces the stars. I have no idea what it means or if I'm just crazier than a loose cannon on the Fourth of July.

I touch my fingers to my cheeks.

"Because other than a silly story about Angelina and Cape in the bedroom, that's all I've heard." I raise my hands up when Darren glances over his shoulder, a smile begging to cut across his lips. It's almost painful to watch him fight it. "And nobody wants to hear about that." I drop my fingers, press my nails into the rough leather of my pants. Night's coming quick, but it's still fairly warm out here, like the air is blushing. A slight heat to touch the cheeks. I smile at my brother and fantasize about changing out of these pants and into a pair of cotton shorts and a tank. *Heaven.*

"I'm not sure what you've heard, but I wanted to clarify

things with you first." I relax into the chair and check out the men that are with my brother today. I know all three of them and they've all got old ladies. I relax a little more. Generally, when there are single guys around, I feel like I'm in the spotlight, like they're all checking me out and trying to decide who I belong to. Right now, I belong to myself. Or if you want to get technical, my brother. It's his name that's on the back of my jacket. I don't want to get pressured into anything. When I decide to give my heart away, I want to make that choice. Even though I'm scared of it, even though I don't know if I'm ready, it has to be mine.

"Okay. Shoot," I tell him as a motorcycle zips by. All the guys turn to look, scoping out the blur of color with critical eyes. As soon as it's out of earshot, they relax a bit.

"We're not trying to start trouble. You know I don't start trouble." I nod my head, drop my chin into my hand and lean on the arm of the chair. The chair that I took because it used to be on the porch of our family home, because I knew my sister was snooping around when I wasn't there, looking for anything of mom's she could find. She'd already snagged a bird house, dug up some of our mother's marigolds, and snatched the welcome mat. The chair was next, I knew it was. Instead of leaving her this as a consolation prize, I removed it from her life completely. It wasn't good enough for me to simply move it inside the house; I had to take it away entirely.

I swallow back the pain and the frustration. It's not all bad. Life isn't all bad. I force my mind back to the present and watch the muscles in my brother's jaw twitch.

"And this isn't a war on women, you know that." Darren turns to look at me fully then, showing me with his eyes what he won't say with his mouth. He loves me, and he'd do anything for me. Except break the rules. Anything except that. "I don't agree with what Bested by Crows did. Not Broken Dallas either. But I also don't like to be disrespected."

My smile gets softer, less jovial. *I knew it.*

"It's okay, Tax. You don't have to tell me that. I know. And I understand."

I watch as he stands up and moves over to me, switching his empty beer bottle from one hand to the other.

"We're not going to hurt anybody, just pay a visit. I should be back by tomorrow evening. Are you going to hang out here or head home?" I shrug, and I have to lick my lips again to keep from asking: *can I come with?* I don't need to see anybody from Triple M in real life. It would only fuel my weird obsession. Instead, I move my gaze to a woman with three little kids trailing behind her, her arms full of brown grocery bags. *Maybe they were triplets? A surprise pregnancy and an even more surprising birth. Her lover passed away in an accident, so she has to raise the children all on her own – while working a nine to five.*

I shiver again and Darren gives me a strange look.

"Thanks for coming to me though, Tax. I know you're just doing what you have to do." My brother gives me yet another tight-lipped smile, and in his gaze, I see something he doesn't want anyone else to see. Darren cares what I think about him, doesn't want me to look at him with anything but respect and love. He's extra careful about what he does.

"You're a good woman, Emilie," he says, bending down for one more kiss on the cheek. When he turns on his heel and leaves the porch, I have to dig my nails into my palms to keep from following after him, from asking what happens when he gets back. *Are we going to talk about me? Are we ever going to talk about me?*

I rise to my feet and stretch my arms above my head, moving over to the railing on the porch and leaning over it just in time to catch a fresh breeze. It rolls off the ocean and teases my nose with salt.

In my head, I start to imagine what it would be like to follow it.

CHAPTER 4

I wake up the next morning madder than a wet hen.

Melissa left me high and dry last night, and I didn't find a damn soul to share my bed with. I knew it. I really do hate the damn beach.

"Toast and fuckin' jam?" I laugh, slapping Gaine in the back of head. "What happened to waking up to a nice cold one?" My friend swipes some dark hair from his face as he glares up at me. Around the edges of his mouth, a smile flits, just waitin' for a word from his sweetheart. I move my gaze over to Mireya and her dark hair, her perfect body, bronzed skin. *Damn, boy, you hit the motherloving jackpot.* If I had to be chained to one woman for the rest of my life, I'd hope she was as hot as Mireya Sawyer.

"Listen, you dick," she says, a slight accent clinging to her lips. "This is as close to a honeymoon as I'm ever going to get, so fuck off and leave us alone." I chuckle as I take a sip of my beer. Mireya rolls her pretty eyes and flips me the bird, returning to her picture perfect little breakfast. This hotel we're staying in is too fancy for my likin'. There were a dozen or more miniature soaps on my bathroom counter this morning, all of 'em in fuckin' French. Boy, I am out of my element here. Gimme a quick spray down and a ride through the countryside and I'm a happy, happy man. But toast and jam? I don't fucking think so.

"Y'all used to be fun. Been married a couple o' days, and you're already gettin' complacent. I might have to whoop your asses into shape." I take another swig of beer and watch as Gaine bites down hard on a piece of toast, smiling as he does it, giving me a look that speaks volumes. He's happy. Fucking happy. I look back at Mireya and then over at Austin and Amy's table. They're all grinning like fools, oblivious to the facts o' life. Oh well. That's why I'm here.

Even if it kills me, I will defend my stupid ass friends to the *death*. That's a mistake I've learned hard and well before. That whole saying, *you don't really miss it until it's gone*. That's truer than a politician's lie. If I lost even a single one of these fuckwads, I'd be a broken man.

"Enjoy your married bliss while it lasts. 'Fore you know it, the two of you will be sexless old biddies, spending your evenings watching the Travel Channel." I slap Gaine in the back and cause him to choke on his fucking tea, laughing my way over to Kimmi's table and plopping down in the empty seat across from her. She doesn't look at me, just keeps her eyes glued to Austin's table. Amy and Christy are sitting next to each other, giggling and perusing a travel guide. It's such a domestic scene, I choke on my beer and have to shake my head to clear it. Peace. I'm almost allergic to it at this point in my life. I grew up with a militaristic daddy, rules instead of hugs, and a mother who acted more like a soldier. Then I joined the military, got discharged, ended up in an MC with more rules than the Marine Corps, and eventually found my way to Triple M. I'm not used to quiet in-betweens, no sir.

But I sure can make jokes about 'em.

"Staring at her tits or her soul, Reynolds? You look like a Goddamn stalker."

"Screw you, Beck," Kimmi says, drawing her green eyes back to mine and raising her beer up. We clink brown glass and drink deep. No omelets or French toast for me and my last, single friend. "What's on your agenda today? Didn't seem like you had much going on last night." I lean back in my chair and match her smile, tooth for tooth.

"Oh, please, Reynolds. When I walked by your room last night, I heard the porn blasting at full volume. Don't pretend your bed was any warmer than mine." Kimmi just sighs and shakes her head, but she doesn't deny my accusations. No point in trying. I know that woman like I know the back of my hand. With a smirk, I set my drink down and run my hands over the front of my leather vest. There's a girl across the room with a book in hand. And on the cover? A biker, baby. *Got this one in the bag.* I scoot my chair back and watch Kimmi glare at me.

"Already tried the bitch. Straight as an arrow."

"Your loss, my gain, sugar pie," I tell her as I stand up and start across the restaurant. The sun is out in force today, sending soldiers of light across the light blue carpeting, the antiqued wooden tables. The dining room is filled with Triple M'ers, but it's quiet in here, calm. Some of it's got to do with the fight with Bested by Crows. There's a subdued quality in the air, and some sorrow, too. Our wounded are well taken care of, though, and we didn't lose a damn man. Not a single fucking one. How's that for bitchin'? Beck Evans knows how to take care of his soldiers.

My fingers itch for a cigarette as I pause next to the table with the curvy brunette.

It takes her a minute to glance up at me, a red straw locked between her teeth as her eyes grudgingly separate from the black text. When she sees me standing there, her eyes go wide as saucers.

I lean forward, putting one hand on the table and my lips just inches from her face.

"You got the time, sweetheart?" I ask as she blinks at me and drops her book to the tabletop. I try not to laugh as the girl fumbles around in her purse, drawing out a cellphone and swallowing a half-dozen times before she actually does get the time out.

"Twelve ... thirty?" she questions as I stand back up, adjusting my red T-shirt and my jeans. I'm not a fancy guy. This is all I wear: my club's colors, a shirt, and jeans. Same pair of boots, day in and day out. And my ink, of course.

That's as close to jewelry or decoration as I'll ever fucking get. Bookworm Lady sets her sights on my knuckles, on the word *Hopeless* spread across my hands.

"You got time for a date?" I ask, rubbing at my chin and missing the goatee. First time in three years I've had a bare face like this. Sure, I got stubble, but it just ain't the same. I'm thirty fucking years old, but this girl don't look like she cares. All she sees are my muscles, my jacket, probably can imagine my bike. I ride a Suzuki Savage – I know, I know, I'm a fucking idiot – so it's not like I got a lot to offer. I used to ride a Harley, an FXDG Disc Glide. It was from 1984. What a fucking dream, man. But I lost that when I left my previous MC to join Triple M. I don't regret it though. And this girl here? She don't give a shit neither. She wants to fuck me as much as I want to fuck her. Then we'll be going our separate ways, and all will be right with the world.

I hold out my hand as she swallows again, setting her book down on the table.

"I'm not really into bikers," she says, and my smile twitches. "My friend lent me this book. I don't really read much either."

Kimmi starts laughing from way off in the distance, and *man*, you could hear crickets chirping.

"Please don't rob me," the girl says as I groan and drop my head back. She clamors to her feet and slaps a twenty down on the table before booking it the hell out of there like she grew up in fucking Crazy Town. Kimmi's laughter is damn near deafening now.

Instead of gettin' pissed about it, I stick a cigarette in my mouth and book it for the back door, pushing through into the sunshine with a slurry of curses. *I really, really hate the beach.* This shit is bull. Haven't had this much trouble finding a lady friend since I outgrew the overalls my daddy used to make me wear to school. *Shoot, son.* Now what?

I head down the street, no particular destination in mind, chuckling as I shake my head at the ridiculousness that is my life.

"Thank you, Jesus," I whisper, letting my cig hang between my lips as I open my arms to the sky and pause next to a travel agency. Even this building is pimped out, covered in pink paint and metal butterflies. Fuck this little fairytale town. I glance down at the brochures fluttering in the wind and reach out to grab one, fingering the shiny paper with rough hands. I ain't about to take no guided tour, but the park it's advertising looks like a nice place for an afternoon. Thing is, do I dare to take a moment to myself? *Nah, nah.* Watch this: second I let my guard down, the shit will rain from the sky. But what I can do is ride around this one horse town and check things out.

I fold the paper up and stick it in my back pocket, turning on my heel and moving down the sidewalk towards the row of gleaming bikes parked out front of our hotel. If you've ever ridden a motorcycle, you understand the pull. I've heard a lot of ignorant folks beg the questions: *why ride a bike when you could have a car? Why ride around with the rain in your face and the sun on your skin*?

My question to them would be: *why the fuck not*?

There is *nothing* in this world that comes close to wrapping your legs around that metal, to taking off into the sunset and wondering where the hell you're going to end up for the night. Feeling the wind in your hair, it's as close to flying as the human race will ever come. Airplanes? What a Goddamn joke. If you can't feel the wind, you're not really living.

I finish my cigarette, stab it out in an ashtray on a nearby garbage can, and move over to my little Savage 650. It's a 2002, but I've taken good care of it, so it still looks brand new. My silver and black baby, my home on wheels, my fucking everything. I rub my hand over the seat and pause with a grin on my face. If I can't have a woman underneath me, I can have this beauty. S'almost as good anyhow.

I mount the love of my life, enjoying the heated feel of the metal, letting the energy of the sun run through my veins as I start the engine. The sound of my bike is almost enough to give me a Goddamn hard-on. *Amen, Jesus, Mother and Mary.* I whip out of the parking space with the sexy screech of rubber on cement and start down the main road, flying past the colorful buildings and the palm trees.

I have no frigging clue where I'm going, but it don't matter much. Part of the fun of the road is *not* knowing where your ass is headed. I spent my whole life *knowing* where I was going, and things didn't turn out right then neither. So why wait in misery?

C.M. Stunich

I take the turn near the beach and go right, heading towards the major highway. I figure if I take this route, ain't nobody going to be able to sneak up on my ass. Besides, it doesn't matter what direction I'm heading or where my final destination is, the wind can still kiss my sunburnt face. The sun can still greet me with bright eyes and a smile. And my bike will still feel like Heaven incarnate.

I take a slow, lazy tour of the town. Granted, there ain't much to see off the main road. Just houses, houses, houses. I don't regret my ride though. Haven't ever regretted a ride. Especially not the one that lead me to Triple M. I used to think of them in a completely different light. I bought into the shit, drank the Kool-Aid, and all that. I was Sergeant at arms for my previous MC. It was my job to keep the guys in line, make sure they followed the rules. If somebody had asked me ten years ago if I'd retire my patch and join a troupe of bank robbing outcasts, I'd have laughed in their faces. Yet, here I am. Baking in the Southern sun and wishing like hell for some of my grandma's catfish. Strange, ain't it? You can take the man out of the South, but you can't take the South out of the man.

I continue to the edge of town, where the exit meets the main road, and then I circle back. I make sure to take my time, to troll the road that meets the beach, to trace the small side roads that pepper the city. No matter where we're at, I do my best to get a lay of the land. Gaine and Austin seem to be operating under some belief that I am a freak of nature, unbeatable, invincible, capable of taking down any enemy. But that ain't true. I'm just a paranoid man with experience, a man who still has the will to keep trying.

I circle the town a few times, repeating every street on my route at least twice. If shit does go down, which it always does, I gotta make sure I'm prepared for it. Ain't nobody else going to be. They've all got other things to worry about. I won't lie either; I *like* defending my family. Get a huge kick out of that shit.

"And what the hell have we got here?" I ask myself as I pause on a small side street, killing my engine and taking note of the white and blue patches that are approaching on the highway. *What the fuck is this?*

Tease

CHAPTER 5

I wake up the next morning with a start.

My heart is pounding again, drawing out a rhythm in my chest that I've never heard before, a song that's never been played. I place my hand against the bare skin above my breasts, listening to the *thump, thump, thump* of my heart. I had that dream again, the one where I was soaring above the earth, swimming through the stars. At the last second, the very moment before I woke up, I saw the arm of the tree and went towards it. But I didn't make it. For the third night in a row, I didn't make it.

I push myself out of bed, letting my feet hit the cool wood floor as I take in my surroundings. I'm not at the clubhouse anymore, but at home. In the house my parents left to my brother, the place he never stays but where I've always lived. My older sister, Lizzie, used to live here, too, but not anymore. She chose to leave this life far behind, scarcely sparing a glance behind her. I both understand and despise my sister's rabid fervency. She wanted a chance to be free, to be able to expand and excel in all categories – not just where my brother said she could. And I could join her at any moment.

I run my hands down my face and yawn.

I never would leave the club. I don't know that I'm even capable of surviving without them. All I have to do is try and imagine what life I might lead. I can't even put together a fantasy that makes sense. It's not the same as when I dream about strangers. This, this is my life, and it's neither a nightmare nor a dream but something in-between.

I shake off the cobwebs of sleep and climb into the shower, rinsing away the last remnants of my dream. My mother used to tell me that dreams meant something, that they always had something to teach us. My dad never believed her, my brother either. So neither did I. Maybe that's why my dad was always disappointed in me? When there's a decision to be made or a stance to be taken, I always go the easy route. I look up to those two men, so whatever they say, I say. Once again, not something I'm proud of. It's just a fact of my life.

I stare into the mirror, using a faded towel to dry my red hair. When it's wet, it reminds me that much more of blood, making me think of my mother. That's not to say she died in an accident or anything. There wasn't even any blood that I could see – not from her or my father. They both died relatively peaceful deaths. It's just, her hair was a shade darker than everyone else's, just a shade. Staring into my eyes like this, it's almost as if I'm looking into her face again. I move my lips and listen to her voice in my head.

Everything has a purpose, Emilie. Even dreams. But nobody can interpret them for you. Only you know what's buried deep inside your own heart.

"Ugh." I get chills up and down my spine, despite the humid heat of the bathroom. Imagining strangers is fine, but when it comes to my own family, it's almost creepy. I turn away and approach the mirror, wiping off the condensation and staring out past the yard and towards the highway. I can just barely make out the stripe of gray in the distance. Darren will have left already, might already be in the process of confronting Triple M. If everything goes according to plan, he'll be back in time for dinner and the only thing that might suffer is some pride. My brother doesn't care if they ride motorcycles or rob banks – we don't unnecessarily climb into other folks' business. What he cares about is if they do it around here, anywhere within driving distance of our hometown. That, and he doesn't want them parading around pretending to be a motorcycle club.

Tim is probably right: *I bet they take their cuts.* If things get really bad, I could see the boys getting into a scuffle. They killed *a lot* of men in Bested by Crows, and they fucked around with Broken Dallas. While Seventy-seven Brothers has no affiliation with either club, Darren might see that as a sign of disrespect. I twist my fingers together and try not to be nervous. I hardly see Darren as things stand anyway.

Once a month, if I'm lucky. And he lives club business, breathes it in instead of air. This is all he does, all the time. So why is this particular item on the agenda getting my heart palpating and my hands sweating? Maybe because I know he's going to ride with the boys, even though he shouldn't. He hides himself in the back sometimes, but only on business he feels personally vested in. That doesn't happen often. *Poor Triple M*. They better watch themselves. I almost feel sorry for them.

"Get over yourself, Tease," I say as I take a step back and move into the bedroom, dressing in a loose fitting shirt and a pair of jeans. When I'm around the guys, I dress like the name implies: corsets, leather pants, dark lipstick. When I'm alone, I'd rather lounge around in a faded gym shirt from my freshman year of high school and my sister's abandoned jeans, just a size too big for me.

I grab my magazine from last night and a pack of cigarettes and head out onto the front porch for some more people-watching fun. Our house is exactly ten blocks away from the clubhouse, along the same street. It's also a historic district, so we get tons of tourists, cameras flashing, eyes wide with wonder. Even our house is a relic from times past. There's a circular placard to the left of the front door. *The Marston House*: *built circa 1719.*

I curl up in a chair, cigarette pressed tight between my lips and start watching, flicking my eyes down to the page every now and again, just to pretend I'm actually reading. Maybe, if I'm lucky today, I'll actually see somebody worth

C.M. Stunich

looking at.

CHAPTER 6

I don't wait around to see what's what. This shit ain't coincidence, and I highly doubt that Seventy-seven Brothers is just stoppin' into town for a nice vacation. I can absolutely guarantee that they are not here for toast and jam.

"I hate being right, Goddamn it." As predicted, here we go again. Another MC, another tussle. I flip my bike around and use those side streets I just memorized to zip back to the hotel. If Seventy-seven Brothers takes the exit from the highway, it'll take 'em about five minutes to catch up to us. Meaning, we can't really get nowhere, not with everybody spread all about, lounging on the fucking beach and whatever. We can make a stand though. I doubt the two cops that patrol this town have enough manpower to stop us.

When Kent was around, he made friends in weird places. Don't know how the man did it. Guess he had some sort of scary charisma or somethin'. I, myself, was immune from the start, but I was drawn to Gaine and Austin, Kimmi, like we'd been friends forever. Anyhow, whatever he did to keep us out of this sort of situation, it'd be nice to know. Startin' fights with other gangs is not my idea of a good time. Yes, I like to rough fuckers up every now and again, but the danger factor here is too high. One wrong move, one misspoken word, and that could be all it takes.

I hop off my bike and burst into the back door of the restaurant, sweating up a storm but trying my best to keep my calm. No need to get these touristy folks up in a tizzy. Luckily, my instincts are dead-on as usual – the lovebirds are still a nestin'. Austin sees me first, standing up from the table with pursed lips and eyes locked on mine.

"We got a problem, Pres. A big one." I put a cigarette into my mouth and light up. Think there's a no smoking thing going on in here, but fuck 'em. What are they going to do? Arrest me? "To be precise with y'all, I'd say we had, I don't know, seventy-seven of them."

"Fuck," Austin snaps, making Christy jump. Poor little blonde belle. I wish we could've welcomed her and Amy under different circumstances, into the world we used to know, where everything was quiet and all our jobs were kept secret behind closed doors. I know it don't sound perfect, but it was nice. It worked. "Where are they?"

"'Bout five minutes out. And they've got all the cavalry onboard. I don't remember how much I told you about Seventy-seven Brothers, but they always ride with seventy-seven members when they're out on club business. *Always*. But that ain't all of them, so we better play real nice here." I glance over at Gaine as he rises from his seat. "No shots fired, you stupid motherfucking asshole." My friend's face flushes, but he doesn't argue. He knows you do stupid shit when you're in love.

"Gaine, sweep the halls and grab anybody you can find. I split the group in half, so there should be at least twenty-five people still here in the hotel. The rest will be out by the beach most likely, so start makin' some phone calls." Austin copies me and sticks a cigarette in his mouth while I grin like a fool and slap Mireya on the back. She scowls at me.

"Finally acting like a real President there," I whisper, watching as Austin turns to Amy with a look. Splitting the group in two, one for leisure time, the rest on guard duty. I love it. Our two Southern belles have already caught the drift and follow Gaine out of the restaurant and into the lobby. Me, I check my weapons one more time and head back outside, fetching one of my pistols from the lock box on the back of my bike. "Please don't kill anybody today, sugar tits," I tell Melissa when she steps out into the sunlight, blinking rapidly as her eyes adjust to the brightness.

"Don't tempt me, Evans," she whispers, moving up next to me and pausing with a hand on one hip. Even after all the shit that went down with Bested by Crows, we never had a security talk. And you know, maybe that was my fault. I should've brought it up before, but we all been through so many changes as of late that my brain's scrambled up like this morning's eggs. Still, we're better prepared here, now, than we were for Broken Dallas and Bested by Crows at the hotel. We'll get the hang of it eventually, I guess. It's adapt or die at this point.

I touch my .38 reverently and then tuck it into my pants. I ain't gonna use the damn thing, but it's there just in case. No such thing as being over prepared.

I close my eyes and listen to the sound of engines in the distance, like the roar of a jet plane taking off. It is that fucking loud, but it's also a thousand times more pleasant. There's a life, a voice, to the sound of those motors running. I lick my lips and taste salt and wind, opening my eyes and scanning the street. I've looked it up and down twice already, but like I said, no such fucking thing as being over prepared. If I know where to stand, how to hide, how to move, I can take on any threat. This is the magic behind the scenes, the things Gaine, Austin, and Kimmi won't ever know about me. I should be teaching them, maybe, but it's hard. I don't know if it's something I could even instill in them or anyone else. I was *raised* like this. It's a part of my DNA.

I stretch my arms above my head, leather vest crinkling as I pull my cig from my mouth and yawn, tossing it down to the pavement with a sigh. No ladies and no rest. Some vacation, right?

"What'd you do last night?" I ask Mel, knowing that nobody but me would bring this shit up right before a confrontation. That's how I roll, though. Like a fast hog down a slow hill. Don't make no sense, but that's me. Pretty sure the universe has been trying to figure out what to do with me forever and a day.

"I sat in my room and I read a book," Melissa says, which is the absolute last thing I ever thought I'd hear her say. I glance over, at her face which is still pretty but etched with fine lines. She's tired, I know she is. And grieving. But she looks better today, just a smidgen. "Amy gave it to me, and I swear to God, it's the hottest sex I've had in years." I grin at her, nice and wide.

"Shoulda let me come in there and help you out with those lady blue balls, my friend. What, you don't like me anymore?" I give her a faux pout as Triple M'ers start to pour out from the building, walking nice and casual but with muscles taut and drawn. I know they're still wary of Austin as the Pres, especially since it kind of just happened and nobody fucking talked about it. I get it. But I also know they see in him what I see. Otherwise, they wouldn't be here. We've had a handful of deserters, but less than I can count on two hands, so I know this can work. All we have to do is find our little niche in this community. We might not be able to get back what we had before, but we can find something new. It's all about riding out the storm. And if there's one thing I know we're all good at, it's fuckin' ridin'.

"Let's make this a peaceful exchange. We're not in their actual territory, just close to it. Nobody owns this beach." Austin comes out of the building with Kimmi by his side. I don't see Gaine or Mireya, so I figure they got stuck babysitting again. I try not to grin too wide. "And we're not here to start trouble. We're just passing through." I watch as Austin takes a deep breath and pulls himself together as the first bikes come around the corner.

Seventy-seven Brothers isn't riding hard, just leisurely sliding into view. Doesn't surprise me. What's the rush, right? They are more than a match for us. If they wanted to mow us all down, they could. I'd make sure they lost a lot of blood first, but it would be inevitable.

At the helm is a man with three 'V' shaped sergeant stripes on the front of his vest. *Sergeant at arms then.* I don't look for their President. Believe it or not, most of the time you never see the stupid fuckers. Austin, Kent, Tray – they're anomalies. Presidents of clubs too small to matter much. When you've got a club this big, the President is kept behind locked doors. Besides, why get your hands dirty when you got others to do it for ya?

The bikes pull up in front of us, a much more cohesive unit than our mixed bag o' tricks. Everybody looks perfect, polished. Their rides are so fuckin' clean, they look like they belong in a Goddamn showroom. And they're all American built choppers. Every last one of them done up in silver, white, and blue. *Hot damn.*

I glance over at Austin, but his face is neutral, carved from stone into a pleasant enough expression. Shoot, he looks like he's about to take a stroll on the damn beach.

The men in the other club cool their rides down, pausing

right there in the center of the road. God help anybody who comes down here now. We ain't movin'.

"Are you Austin Sparks?" the Sergeant at arms asks, climbing off his ride and pausing in the sunshine, dark hair reflecting back the sun like a mirror. His cool, blue eyes sweep the group, and a smile lights his face. It's not entirely unpleasant, but there's something creepy about it, too.

"I am," Austin says, taking a step forward and holding out his hand. The man looks down at it and moves forward, grabbing hold tight and shaking firmly. "What can I help y'all with?" The sergeant at arms takes a step back and glances over his shoulder, letting his eyes move down the row of men straddling their choppers. None of the others bother to climb off. I take it they don't plan to stay long. That's a good thing, though. I sniff the air and taste a hint of violence on the back of my tongue. If we stay calm, handle this thing well, maybe we'll be alright. I take a wide stance and wait with my chin up, a slight smirk on my face.

"Well, you see. We're here to ask you a few, small favors. Now, it's up to you to decide if you're going to do them for us. You say no, we say okay. But then there's a game changer. See, then the favors become fervent requests. And after that, well. You don't really want to know what comes after that." The man smiles with his small teeth. I don't like the look of 'im. Not one fucking bit. He's got pale blue eyes and a sense of entitlement. In another life, this man would be an ex-frat boy, working a nine to five and cheatin' on his wife. He hardly looks like he could be the Sergeant at arms for an MC as big as this one. Guess looks can deceive.

"We'll see what we can do. What exactly did you have in mind?" Austin asks, keeping his stance relaxed. His sandy hair ruffles a bit in the breeze but otherwise, he's completely still. The man facing him glances over his shoulder again, takes another look at his men.

"It's real easy," he says, turning back again, letting his attention fall to the Triple M'ers on either side of Austin. "Hand in your cuts, gather your people and take a hit."

"Excuse me?" Austin asks, dropping his arms by his sides. *Aw, shit.* I move forward, but not a lot, just enough to make the other side nervous but not spook the crap out of 'em.

"Take a hit from me to make up for the disrespect you've shown us by coming through here without permission, for committing thefts against communities we consider ourselves a part of, and for the deaths of the men you've taken on your way here. Three simple things is all we ask. And when you're done, you can leave."

"You have got to be motherfucking kidding me?" Austin says, his voice *this* frigging close to violence. "You want our jackets? You want to fucking *punch* me? In front of my club?" Murmurs and snarls break out on our side. Respect. It goes a long way in this life, especially for people like us, people who choose to view life from a different angle. We don't collect fancy cars or houses, horde money, make investments. We travel the road, collect sights and sounds instead. Respect and pride are practically currency here.

And now we're being asked to pay a massive debt?

I lick my lips and get ready for shit to start. They aren't going to kill us, not unless we take it to that level, but this is going to hurt.

"What's it going to be, Mr. Sparks?" the Sergeant asks, lifting his chin up and waiting in the peaceful silence of a summer afternoon. I look over at Kimmi's stern face, let my gaze move back over to Mel's stoic expression.

"I'm sure you already know what my answer's going to be," Austin growls. It's then that I expect the blows to start, for weapons to be drawn from pockets, for yet another fuckin' scuffle. I don't expect to hear a shot fired, a burst of sound that shakes me to my core. A spray of wetness that splatters my face and drops Melissa to her knees.

Somebody just shot Melissa fucking Diamond. From behind.

Beck

CHAPTER 7

My mind rips to shreds as I explode forward, sliding to my knees on the ground next to her. She's still alive, that much I can tell, even as my eyes scan the buildings around us looking for a shooter. But whoever it was only fires the single shot.

"Oh, come now, Mel. You can't go like this," I growl out as I touch her cheek. She's coughing and groaning, bleeding out from her midsection. I touch my hand to the wound, try to stifle the bleedin'. But I ain't gonna be able to do much for her. I have to get her to a fuckin' hospital.

I look around, snatching the attention of a fellow Triple M'er. I have to help Mel, but I also can't leave my other friends high and dry.

"Put pressure on her wound," I snarl at the man; Christopher is his name. He's been in the club as long as I have. I know I can trust him with my friend. I pass Mel over and rise to my feet, blood surging hot and fiery through my veins. My vision blurs a bit as I pull the gun from my pocket and raise it up, aiming it on the first man in blue and white that I find. *Fucking pussies.* I don't expect a lot from people, but I demand some Goddamn pride and dignity. I thought Seventy-seven Brothers was at the very least a respectable club. Not anymore. Not any-fucking-more.

I line my shot up and fire, just once, moving onto the next guy in line. Anybody that has a gun, I'm going to shoot to kill. Sorry, didn't want it to go this way, but I was pushed. I lock onto that cold calmness that comes when you're drenched in shit and ain't goin' nowhere. It's that shield that falls into place that protects the heart, at least for that single moment in time. What nobody bothers to tell ya is that once you're alone in bed at night, the feelings you got rid of before come rushing straight back, slamming into you and knockin' you silly. They all move in at once – with a motherfucking vengeance.

A smile tweaks my face as I fire off another round, drop another man. A split second later, I'm jamming my elbow into a man's face as he comes up beside me, a wrench in one hand. It's the Sergeant. *Well, hot damn.* I force my gaze to stay off the spot I left Melissa, turning to the guy with the blue eyes and the ugly smile. I don't bother to level the gun on him; he's too fucking fast, getting into my space as I drop my weapon to the ground and reach out to intercept him, throwing him against my bike hard as I can. He comes right back at me, nearly a foot shorter but a hell of a lot tougher than I'd have given him credit for.

I don't get the chance to deck him one that he deserves because there's another guy on my right, two more on my left. Shitty thing about numbers: seventy-seven to twenty-five, even forty-four if we were all here and able-bodied, doesn't make good odds. I slip the hammer from my pocket and swing it around, hitting a blonde in the side of the head with it. The crack that follows is fucking sickening. I just grin wider, keep that smile on my face as long as I can. It can protect me the way nothing else could. I kick out and smash the other man hard as I can in the kneecaps. Dropping down, I slam my body into the Sergeant as he comes at me again, wrench still clutched firmly in his hand. When he falls to his back on the pavement, I don't hesitate in drawing my knife, falling to my knees in front of him. Having military training comes in handy sometimes. Every once in a great while, you get to kill the bad guy.

I thrust my knife into the man's gut, smiling while I do it. Breaking inside. I pull my blade out and hit him again, and again, and again. One more time for good measure, splattering my face with more red, staining my devil driven heart a darker shade of black. Without waiting around to see what he does, I surge to my feet and swing into another group of Brothers. I unleash the motherfuckin' beast and pray to God I can at least get my friends out of here alive. I don't have time to look around and check on them. The odds, even for me are overwhelming. If everybody in Triple

M had been where I've been, this would be a piece of cake. As things stand, I'll be lucky to find out that some folks were at least able to hold their own.

I swing my hammer like a fucking sword, smashing the metal into the bodies of the men around me, their black jackets and blue colors a blur to my wild vision. Beck Evans takes a break sometimes, steps out of his body and lets the animal take over. Right now, that animal is furious. I spin around and through a gap in the melee, I see the bloodstained spot where Mel had been laying. But she's not there anymore. Christopher is, but he isn't fucking moving. I look around, my eyes scanning the gathered crowd as quick as I can. I manage to find Kimmi and Austin, but I don't see Mel anywhere. If she could get up and fight, I'm sure she would, but I don't see 'er. I do not fuckin' see 'er.

"Mel!" I shout, shoving back another guy, moving into the street. I hate fights like this, where chaos is erupting and exploding all around you. I feel like I'm floatin' above the damn ground, peering down at this gathered crowd o' fools. "Mel!" I don't see nothing, and I don't hear nothing that gives me a clue as to where she might be. But I do see lights at the end of the street, red and blue. Two cop cars wait at the intersection in the road, near the beach. They don't bother to do shit at this point. I mean, hell, what the fuck they gonna do? Fight a hundred plus bikers with stun guns and rubber bullets? *Shoot, man.*

You can bet though that they're calling in reinforcements. *Fuck and shit.*

"Austin!" I shout, turning back to the melee, wading into a group of jackets and grabbing a man by the hair. Around me, I can hear the sound of motors. Most of the Triple M'ers are climbing onto their rides. I toss the man to the side, using his hair to send him rolling onto the pavement as I come up to my Pres.

"Get on your fucking bike, Beck. We're getting the fuck out of here." Austin is breathing hard and blood is running down his face, but he looks alright. "I just sent Kimmi up for the others. At this point, we've got to go. I'm spreading the word to run. We'll meet up on the highway. If you see the cops, keep going and we'll find each other later. Go."

"Where the fuck is Mel?" I demand, noticing that we're not the only ones pulling back. Seventy-seven Brothers knows what a few cop cars now can mean later. With all the shit we been pullin', I would not be surprised to see an entire SWAT team. *Fuckin' shit.* "Where is she?" I scream when Austin doesn't answer. He gives me a look that says he don't know crap, and turns his attention to getting the group together. Me, I move forward and try to catch sight of the men leaving on their bikes. They aren't going to let this go, not after that bloodbath. I'm about to give up and go after Austin when I see her.

Melissa.

Fuck! I run forward as fast as I can and hop on my bike. There's not a fucking second to spare. For whatever fucking reason, fate or whatnot, I ain't got the slightest, somebody from Seventy-seven Brothers has got Melissa on their ride.

They're taking my wounded friend, but why? Well, to make sure we pay. That's fucking why. If they take her, we can either leave our friend to a fate worse than death or we can follow after.

I am bound and motherfucking Goddamn determined to take that advantage away from them.

"Beck!" Austin screams after me, but I'm already kicking away from the curve and flying down the road, chasing blue and white and broken dreams.

Tease
CHAPTER 8

I decide to devote my entire day to people-watching, waiting for the sun to set in the sky and remind me that I should head to the clubhouse sooner rather than later. I'm going to spend as much time with my brother as I can before he disappears to God only knows where. I'd had plans to clean up the house, maybe get some paint for the living room. It's looking less than ideal in there. My mother passed away midway through her renovation of the old house, so some rooms, like the kitchen, are near perfect. Others, like the living room need some work. I'm not much of a do-it-yourselfer, but I think I'm capable of throwing up a coat of pale yellow paint. But instead of doing that, I'm still sitting here fantasizing about the lives of strangers.

Today's crowd is a lot more interesting than usual. I've seen a man in clown makeup, a lady with no shoes, and three separate groups of Japanese tourists. I'm starting up another cigarette and smiling at a pair of girls in matching pink T-shirts when I hear the sound of a bike coming my way. Not many riders come down this street – anyone that knows their shit knows Seventy-seven Brothers has their clubhouse here. Occasionally we get a rider or two who has no idea who we are, who doesn't even know there's an entire world buried below the surface of their lives. Leisure riders, folks who own a motorcycle but have nothing to do with any club. My brother doesn't mind these people, but what he does mind are full patched riders sliding through his territory.

The cigarette tumbles from my lips and hits the denim of my jeans. I swipe at it and knock it to the floor where it crackles and burns, a single spot of orange in the shadows of the porch. I'm not looking at it though. I can't. The only thing I'm capable of staring at is the insanity that's going on right in front of me. A rider blasts down our street, sliding to a stop directly in front of the house, tires skidding across the pavement, burning the road with the hot scent of rubber.

I stand up and move towards the railing, curling my fingers around the old wood. Inside my chest, my heart beats a broken rhythm of surprise. I felt both light-headed and grounded at the same time. The air in my lungs becomes stagnant when I forget to breathe. I blow it out in a rush and suck in a massive breath, letting my chest get tight with sunshine and sweet ocean air.

What … what happened today? I wonder as the man climbs off his bike, his entire face and torso splattered with red. He's wearing a leather vest with patches on the front. One of them says *MFFM*. My brother's club wears one like that, too. *BFFM*. It means *Brothers Forever, Forever Brothers*. I can't be sure what his means, but I can take an educated guess. *M Forever, Forever M*. Triple M. This man is from Triple M.

I stagger back a step when his eyes find mine, green boring into green. Through the red splatters on his face, I see tracks like tears. We stand there for a long moment, my heart still racing, his fists clenching tight at his sides. That's when I realize I've made a really stupid fucking mistake. *I'm wearing my jacket.* It got chilly out earlier as a cloud passed over the sun and cut through the beautiful day. I was so entranced with the lady with no shoes on that I just grabbed the first thing hanging on the coat tree.

My brother always warns me about wearing club colors at the house. Usually, there are guys hanging around here just in case, but today, there aren't any. Most of the club went out to meet Triple M, and the rest are at the clubhouse. They might only be blocks away, but that's ten blocks too far. I've made it eighteen years without getting into any shit with another MC. Looks like my lucky streak is up.

I start to move back, realizing too late that this redheaded demon staring straight at me is serious trouble. *Triple M.* I can see the letters tattooed on his massive bicep. He's so magnetic, I'm having a hard time drawing my gaze away. Down below, my body stirs, tightening places low. Unconsciously, I run my tongue over my lips, even as I start to run, as I reach for the handle on the screen door.

Footsteps pound behind me, unbelievably fast, almost inhumanly quick. I think then that maybe I made a *second* mistake. I just turned around and flashed the rockers on the back of my jacket. *Property of Tax. Seventy-seven Brothers.* It's all right there, whatever evidence this man needed to make his decision.

His hand wraps around my hair and drags me back a step, ripping my fingers painfully from the handle of the door.

"Who are you to them?" he growls at me, yanking my head so far back that I can see his face, dripping with sweat, cutting more tracks through the dried blood. His voice is broken and his eyes wild. We're both breathing fast, chests rising and falling at the same rate. My fingers slide down my pants, searching for a weapon. In the front left pocket, I've got a small knife. As I swallow hard and dig my fingers under the denim, I try to answer him.

How this guy got down here without anybody seeing, I don't know. But if I can hold him back from whatever he's planning on doing for just a few minutes, somebody from the club is bound to drive by and see us grappling here on the porch. Hell, even a normal citizen walking by would probably call the police. The man's a bit spooked. I can tell; his eyes are darting this way and that. He's probably wondering why he found me here. After all, it doesn't take a genius to figure out that he was looking for the clubhouse.

"Are you his ol' lady?" the redhead snarls, drawing me

back further. My hair is embedded in his tattooed knuckles and pain is shooting through my skull. In my eyes, I see stars silhouetted against the brightness of the sun. I run my tongue over my lips again and try to speak.

"Who?" My voice is crooked, weak from the angle of my neck. And the pain ... I'm the first to admit that I've led a fairly charmed life. This is probably the most physical pain I've ever been in.

"Sergeant at arms. Your Sergeant at fucking arms. Are you his ol' lady?"

"No," I whisper as I finally get my fingers wrapped around the hilt of the knife. "I'm Tax's sister." And then I swing my hand back, aiming for his thigh. A massive hand grabs my wrist, fingers curling so tight around my skin that I cry out and drop the knife. The man lets go of my hair and spins me around, shoving me hard into the wall of the house, right underneath the historical plaque. His green eyes are devastatingly gorgeous, a well of color and emotion. A shade that echoes my own, like we speak the same language through our gazes. My knees feel weak as hot breath brushes over my face, making my eyes flutter closed. *What is wrong with me?* Something about this whole MC is getting me deep down. I didn't know anything about them, and I was having visceral reactions to the stories. Why? As I stand there with the massive stranger towering over me, I think I know why. I don't want to admit it to myself, but I get a niggling in my belly. *You want to belong, but maybe, you don't want to belong here?*

I shake the blasphemous thought away as my eyes fly open, and I spit into the redhead's face. I don't know what he's going to do to me, but whatever it is, I'll be okay. I can get through this. On the outside, I might seem weak, but on the inside, I'm strong.

"Tax?" he whispers, ignoring my insult. "Why you wearin' a property patch if you're his fucking sister?" The man's voice is faraway, like maybe he's only here in body and not soul. Whatever happened today, whoever's blood that is, it hurt him bad. *What did you do, Darren*? *And are you okay*? *Please be okay.* "Doesn't matter. I don't fuckin' care." The man shifts his shoulder forward and uses the fabric on his T-shirt to wipe away some of the sweat and my spit from his face. "You're comin' with me, sweetheart."

"Fuck I am," I blurt at him, doing my best to come up with a plan. I'm shoeless which is a huge hindrance. I could kick at him, but it probably wouldn't do me any good. My brain spins as I think up a hundred different scenarios. My brother's taught me how to defend myself. Today's just been a mix-up of strange circumstances and poor mistakes. *And this odd ache in my belly. This weird connection to the bastard towering over me.* I suck in a massive breath and get ready to scream.

I hardly get out a squeak before I'm being tugged forward by my wrists and have a gun pressed into my belly. My captor presses his forehead to mine, closing his eyes and sighing heavily, like the weight of the world is on his shoulders.

"I do not want to shoot you, sugar cakes. But if I have to, I will. I'm sorry, but I'll do it, and I won't look back."

The man opens his green eyes and locks gazes with me, stealing my breath away, knocking the sense from my head. He releases my wrists and steps away, gesturing down the steps with his gun. I could keep fighting here; my brother would probably respect me more if I did. But I can tell on this guy's face: he's serious. He'd put that bullet in me and walk away twice as broken as he is now. I don't want to die facedown on this porch. I can't. It's just not the way things are supposed to be.

Besides, I know from his look, the deep set of his frown, the tightness of the skin on his face, that whatever happened back there, Seventy-seven Brothers burned him hard. *Oh, no, no, no, no. This was not supposed to happen. It wasn't* supposed *to happen.*

Or maybe, just maybe, in some grand scheme of the universe, it *was.*

Tease CHAPTER 9

Once I'm situated on the front of the redhead's bike, I don't bother to fight. As someone who grew up around bikes could tell you, a crash on one of these things *hurts*. There's nothing between you and the road, but a bit of leather. Or today, in my case, some old jeans. My flesh would be stripped from my bones if we were to take a fall. So no, I don't fight, but I think about it. About what I'm going to do when we stop.

Right now, I've got the wind in my face, and my heart in my throat. It's still pumping furiously, reminding me that a couple hundred pounds of rock hard muscle is wrapped around my body. I am keenly aware of his scent, a mixture of blood, sweat, and some sort of spicy soap that gives me the chills. I want to be sitting here hating him, but I can't find it in me. Obviously, something happened to him, something that my club was responsible for. I don't see malice in his eyes or lust or greed, just frustration and fear. Besides, if he'd wanted to hurt them, he could've simply killed me. There's another motive here.

I swallow hard and listen to the rapid thumping of this man's heart. It's pressed tight against my back, beating a rhythm that's a near perfect match to mine. We're both worked up, pumped full of adrenaline and breathing hard. For one of the first times in a long time, I get to ponder the question: *what the hell happens next*?

We move down the highway at a blistering speed, right up until a series of red and blue lights flashes by us on the opposite side of the divider wall. I feel the man behind me tense and then all of a sudden, we're flying down a ramp and into a suburban area I know I've been to before. We maneuver through the area at lightning speed, racing around slow moving minivans and slipping right out of the clusters of houses and perfect yards and into the countryside.

We haven't been traveling for more than an hour when suddenly, we're pulling sharply onto the gravel shoulder of the road and stopping on a dime. The redhead gets off of the bike and takes a few steps back from me, putting his hands on the back of his head and breathing in sharply.

"Shoot and fuck and Goddamn it, Mother Mary and Christ the Lord. *Why*?"

He screams his frustration into the quiet air, getting some very strange looks from a herd of nearby cows. I know he's still got the gun on him, so I stay put on the motorcycle, watching as he moves in a small circle and then pauses, drawing a cellphone from his pocket. He dials a number, waits. Hangs up. Tries again. "Fuck a pig," he growls, squeezing the phone in his hand for a moment before reconsidering and sticking it back in his pocket.

Then he pauses for a moment and just stares at me. I get that strange feeling in my stomach again, that pull that makes me wish I could step off the bike and move across the gravel towards him. Towards my *kidnapper*. Towards a member of a rival gang, one that might possibly have hurt my brother. I touch a hand to my chest and listen to the beat of my heart through my fingertips.

"What's your name, sweetheart?" he asks me. The wind picks up for a moment, blows my red hair around my face and sticks it to my lips. I consider not answering him, but what will that gain me? The club will know I'm missing sooner rather than later, and they'll come looking for me. If negotiations aren't made first. He'll learn my name somehow, someway. Anyway, I might stand a better chance escaping this unscathed if I make him look at me as a person and not an object to be bartered with.

"Tease." I pause and then add, "Or Emilie Hathorne." The man stands there staring at me for a long, long moment, his own red hair whirling around in the breeze. After a moment, he takes out a cigarette and puts it between his lips.

"Beck Evans." He takes a drag and then drops it, crushing it out with the heel of his boot.

"What are you going to do to me, Beck?" I ask, not liking the way the question comes out. *Almost like a come-on.*

"My brother is extremely possessive of me. Right now, you're risking your life having me here. As soon as he finds us, he'll kill you."

"Bring it on, baby," Beck says, his voice rough, strained to the edge of breaking. "That's sort of the idea here anyhow. For him to find us. Soon as he does, he gives me back my friend." Beck shrugs. "I give 'im back his sister." I start to turn slightly in my seat, but stop when Beck puts his hand on his gun.

"Tax. My brother. He's the President of Seventy-seven Brothers." I debated with myself, on whether or not I should admit this. But I think it might help my cause. Beck will know I'm worth something for sure. I'm not just an old lady, a bitch for one of the members to keep in his garage, clean his bike, serve his food. I'm blood related, protected over, guarded.

"Well, your brother is a damn fool," Beck growls out, pulling out his phone again, dialing another number. From the look on his face, still no answer. "If he hadn't given the order to shoot my friend, neither of us would be standing here right now. We might have a couple o' black eyes and some wounded pride, but that would be it. Sugar, your fucking family is going to wish they were dead if they touch one finger to Mel. If she dies on their watch, boy, am I going to lose my shit."

"What did you do?" I ask him because Darren would never just shoot someone, let alone a woman. In fact, I'm finding myself hard-pressed to imagine a single scenario where my brother would ever condone that. And I know he was there. He said he was going out on this ride today. "What did you do to my family?" I stand up as Beck moves forward, sliding a knife from his pocket and pointing it at my throat.

"I didn't do *shit*," he growls, grinding his teeth together. I know it's a terrible moment to say this, but ... he has nice lips. A full bottom curve and a bow tie up top. I swallow and lean away from the blade. "We were standing there havin' a nice chat when one of your pussy Brothers shot Melissa fuckin' Diamond right through the back. This is *his* fault, your piece of shit, pansy ass, loser of a brother."

"Fuck you!" I scream because Darren is *not* like that. *We* are not like that. Seventy-seven Brothers doesn't *do* things like that. "We would never disrespect another club like that, not unless they'd pushed all our buttons first, threatened us, hurt one of our own. If Tax ordered that, then you must be horrible fucking people." Beck leans back and tucks his knife away, squeezing his fists so hard, the veins in his hands stand out sharply against his skin. He looks like he wants to hit me, and that's fine. I'm willing to take one for my brothers and sisters. "Respect, dignity, pride, and family. Those are our credos. What are yours? You steal from others and you kill indiscriminately."

"Indiscriminately? Oh, sugar tits, you are very well misinformed," Beck drawls, leaning back and putting a wicked slash of a smile across his face. "We killed before to protect ourselves, to protect the rights of our women, to fight for the right to live the way we want." Beck shakes his head and takes one more step back, scoping me out from head to toe. I can feel his gaze like it's a physical thing, burning through my clothes, eating me up from the inside. I have to swallow three times before I can even speak.

"There are two sides to every story." I want to ask if my brother is still alive, but I doubt he'd have the answer to that, or if he'd even tell me if he knew. I lean back a little and even though it's not really in my personality, not in my best interest, and certainly a stupid ass fucking thing to do, I check him out. Just the same way he's looking at me.

"All that comin' from an ol' lady? You got a pretty mouth there, lady luck. You want to put it to better use tonight? Pass the time while you wait for your pathetic fuck of a brother to come and barter for your ass?"

"You wouldn't touch me," I tell him, using the judgment of his character to make the assumption. The smile is false, the bravado real. He doesn't want to hurt me, but he will. At the same time, I don't think he'd get any pleasure out of it. "This isn't about me."

Beck's face relaxes up a bit, and he shakes his head.

"No. You're right. This ain't about you at all. I just want to do damage control, get my friend back, find out who the fuck your people took away from me."

"They wouldn't do it without a reason," I repeat, wondering who he and his friends took away from us. Triple M. I was fantasizing about them, and here one of them is, and he's nothing like I expected. *And everything like I did.*

"Keep flappin' your lips and the wind is bound to listen," Beck says, moving forward and pausing a few inches from me. I watch as he puts his hand on his gun. I turn away and stare out ahead of us, at the open road, and I wonder how far this is going to go. If the ending's going to be something I can live with. *Or if there's going to come something I can't live without.*

CHAPTER 10

I don't want to be thinkin' nasty thoughts right now, but I can't help myself. I'm a man, and I'm wrapped around a beautiful woman, a woman whose body is hot and ripe, rounded curves in all the right places. She's got these perfect lips and hair the color o' blood. Better circumstances, better days, and I would've picked her up in a hot second. Right now, I have to worry about my club, my friends. Who the fuck is dead, injured, and where the fuck they all are. I got my cellphone, programmed with the number of everybody in Triple M, but that doesn't do me any good if they don't fucking answer.

Nashville it is then, I guess.

I get to ride for eleven hours with unknowns crawling around in my head, what-ifs and all that. *A shooter on the roof?* It just doesn't seem like something Seventy-seven Brothers would do. And then why just one guy? Why not have a whole host of guys up there waiting to shoot us? I hate this covert ops sort of shit. Why can't everything be plain as Goddamn day? The world would be a lot better place if it were simplified a shade or two.

Melissa, I'm sorry. I tried to keep up with the group, but they split off a few guys and took shots at me while I was riding. It was get hit or stay back, that much was obvious. And then I lost them right as I was coming into town.

Then I saw *her.*

When I first stopped, I didn't even know what I was doing. I saw that shock of red hair, the bright green eyes, so piercing from so far away. There was a pull in the air, like I was being controlled from within, pushed forward against my own will. Strange as shit, I'll tell you that much. Then I saw her jacket, her colors, and I knew what I had to do. If she really is the Pres's little sister, then the hopes of getting Mel back are high. *Provided she doesn't die from that gunshot wound.*

I squeeze my fingers around the handlebars and rocket down the freeway, happy that the wind is fierce enough to hide this girl's sweet scent from me, like a field of flowers or somethin'. *Woo wee, Tease sure is a right appropriate name.* This woman still has me thinking about things I shouldn't be thinking about. Actually, on the other hand, maybe this is exactly what I should have my mind focused on. I can't do anything but ride right now. In another hour or so, I'll pull over and try my friends' phones again. For now, I'm trapped right here with my arms around her and her body pressed tight against me. If my pants get a bit tighter, who would know?

For a second there, I get all nostalgic and start pinin' away for Austin and that horse shit music he likes so much. I start reminiscing about Mireya's snarky commentary and Melissa's overly ridiculous outfits, dark makeup, and blatant come-ons. *This is not over, Beck. Not by a long shot. Stop being a bitch and get your crap together.*

I smile wider and ride harder, grinding my wheels into the hot pavement, letting my sorrows spill from my skin and fly away in the breeze. Back to that cold calmness. I almost let my anger and my fear get the best of me. Almost. But Beck Evans has a lot of practice in this department. I draw on my past mistakes, lessons learned, and I man the fuck up.

By the time we get to the border between North Carolina and Tennessee, I can almost pretend that I don't give a shit.

"Answer your damn phone, you son of a bitch," I growl, leaving a message for Austin first. Then Gaine, Mireya, Kimmi, until I'm halfway through the alphabet with no information and a massive fucking headache. The few folks that pick up don't know shit about shit. Nashville. That's the last thing they heard, so it's where we're all headed. I make plans with anyone I can get ahold of to meet outside the city proper, on the side of the highway. I don't like that I have to ride all the way there, leave Melissa behind, but there's not much else that makes sense at this point. I have to find my MC and scrape us all back into shape. As long as I have this foxy, young thing on my bike, I've got leverage.

"Get off the bike," I snap at Miss Thing, my lips wrapped around a cigarette. She gives me a weird look, staring straight at and through me with those green eyes. They're about the same shade as Kimmi's, as mine. Green, but with flecks of gold instead of brown. Two little clovers right there in that cute as a fuckin' button face. Even with that ugly T-shirt and those loose jeans, I can tell the babe's got a body. After a brief moment of hesitation, Miss Emily 'Tease' Hathorne climbs off and wipes her sweaty palms on the thighs of her jeans. "If we're gonna get to Nashville alive, we gotta eat."

"Eat?" Tease looks back at the diner behind us, silhouetted against the slowly setting sun. Something about summer is just weird to me, like the days aren't really longer, just that the sun takes more time to set, wading through golden light in its quest to escape the sky.

"Yeah, eat," I snap and then force the smile back onto my face. I continue to smoke my cigarette, watching as Tease's eyes catch on the burning cherry. "Listen, darlin', I feel like I been rode hard and hung up to dry. My mouth's as dry as a nun's cunt and it's hotter than a billy goat's ass in a pepper patch. All I want to do is have a damn Coke, a burger, and some fuckin' fries." I flip the cigarette at her and watch in surprise as she manages to catch it, taking a drag and closing her eyes. "But first, take off your jacket."

Tease pauses, glancing around at the mostly empty parking lot. I'm not worried about taking her into the diner. Club business is club business. I know she knows she doesn't stand a snowball's chance in hell if she flaps her lips at the waitress.

"No."

"What the fuck do you mean, *no*?" I growl, moving forward and getting in her face again. I don't mean to be so darn nasty, but hey, my fuckin' life is in shit shambles right now, and this bitch is the enemy. "My grandma taught me manners, missy, but I don't extend courtesies to the enemy. I ask you to take your jacket off, *please*. Last chance."

"Or you'll take it off for me?" she asks, and I almost lose my shit. Hot little redhead asks me to take something off? *Fuck*. I look her up and down again, taking in her creamy soft skin, her long fingers, bright eyes. She's young, probably eighteen, nineteen at the most. I might be a couple o' years older, but I can't say I'd be opposed to playing around. *If only we had the time or leisure.*

"Or yeah, I could make that happen for you. You definitely don't want to tease me. If I want your jacket off, it's coming off." Teases swallows and stares me down. I can tell she's used to following orders, but I'm also the enemy. I know how she's been raised, what she's been told. Typical ol' lady, even if she belongs to her damn brother. *Fucking weird shit going on here.* I bet this girl is going to fight me tooth and nail.

"Then do it," she says defiantly, red lips a shade too dark for her face. I'd like to see them pale and pink, a compliment to her skin instead of a contrast. *Or not. Get your head out of your hard as fuck dick, Beck.* I can feel my cock brushing up against the inside of my jeans. So inappropriate, so out of place. So me. *Forgive me my sins, Melissa, baby.* I will find you. "Right here in this parking lot, in front of all these people. Fight me. I know you can overpower me, and you can get your way, but it's going to cost you."

"I've been a lot of places, seen a lot of things, you sure you want to fight me on this?" Tease stands tall and unapologetic, staring me down with her softly sloping eyes. Naturally, my gaze travels downwards, towards her breasts, but since there ain't nothin' to see, I end up focusing on her collarbone. My eyes trace the fine line there, imagining what would happen if I touched my fingers to it, curled my nails around the gray cotton of that tee and tore it clean off. I sure would like to get my frustrations out right now. I won't force myself on the girl, but if she wants to fight me, a fight is what she'll get.

I reach out and grab her around the wrist, lightning quick. I don't doubt that she's a tough lady. You have to be to exist in this world, whether you're a full patched member like Mireya or an old lady like this chick. But toughness doesn't necessarily prepare a person for my own personal Beck bullshit. I yank Tease forward on her bare feet, pulling her across the gravel without much effort. Her body slams into mine, breasts smashing up against my chest as my arm snakes around her back and grabs hold of the jacket.

My dick gets hard as a rock, grinding painfully against my jeans as I struggle to keep in control of myself.

"Jacket, *off*," I growl into her ear, getting a little too close with my teeth, scraping her skin and sending chills through her body. I can feel her shaking against me, but not out of fear. I've kidnapped the girl, threatened her, and she's not afraid. Either she's just plain stupid or I really do have that magnetic, magical charm I always boast about.

Tease swallows and the sound truly and utterly convinces me that her nickname is a hell of a lot more accurate than her given name. This girl is no *Emilie*.

"No." Tease snatches my knife out of my pocket and slices up towards my bicep, managing to cut into my jacket but stopping short of my flesh. I manage to catch her before any real damage can be done and squeeze her arm so tight she drops this weapon, too.

"I warned you, cupcake," I tell her, wrapping one arm around her waist, the other around her arm. Even as she struggles, I start to move her across the gravel, her feet levitating just *this* much off of the ground. To any onlookers, we're like any other couple havin' a friendly chitchat. Nobody has to know she's not actually walking alongside me. She could fight harder, sure, but then people will come running and I think she knows how desperate I am. Like I said, I *will* shoot her. I don't want to, but I absolutely will. I've done harder things before. You can't always win the war by being the nice guy.

I take Tease around the side of the diner, opposite the highway and slam her into the wall, flipping her around and tearing the jacket from her arms. Immediately, she spins on me, eyes flickering this way and that, contemplating her next move. But she's not impulsive or stupid. Surprising, right? I haven't known many girls her age to have that much sense. Definitely haven't known any boys. I was a fucking idiot when I was her age. Still am, I guess.

I toss the jacket to the ground and step on it.

"Off means off." I get out another cigarette as Tease steps forward and shoves at me. I don't go nowhere, but that doesn't mean the act doesn't annoy me. "We can have a cigarette together, and share lunch. Or I can whoop your ass and put you in your place. Your choice. Remember who's the fucking prisoner here."

"Get your foot off my cut," she says, and her voice is less cherubic and actually a little intimidating. I watch as her fingers curl by her sides. "I haven't disrespected your club; don't disrespect mine."

I take a step forward, both feet now firmly planted on the leather of the jacket. My eyes follow a drip of sweat that falls from Tease's forehead, slides down the curved line of her jaw. Her full lips are trembling and the pulse in her neck flutters. *Hot damn.* I have to actually adjust myself before I move forward, tucking the boys into place best I can.

"Make. Me."

I take a drag on my cigarette and toss it to the side. Tease comes at me again, giving me just enough time to remove my gun and throw it down alongside the still crackling cherry. She goes to shove me again, and I snatch her wrists, holding her body stiff and rigid just inches from mine. Our mouths are so close we could fuckin' kiss.

"Now what?" I ask as she breathes in hard and deep, chest rising and falling in rapid succession. I notice absently that mine's doin' the same. I swallow and wet my lips, feeling the stir of my body down below. I am so fuckin' hard, I could fuck a rock and break it.

Tease stares into my face, body trembling against mine, and then she kisses me. Tears at my lips and smears her red lipstick across my face. My hands release her arms and scramble at her jeans, unbuttoning them in an instant and shoving them down her hips. I am a motherfucking expert at this shit. I'm no good with heart to hearts, apparently no damn good at taking care of my friends. But sex? I can do sex. I step on her jeans and manage to get them the hell out of my way, pushing her up against the wall with my body as she scratches at the back of my neck with her nails. We kiss furiously, tongues tangling, as I keep one hand wrapped around her waist and use the other to free myself from my pants. My dick is so eager, it practically opens the zipper for me, springing free hard and insistent.

I don't bother with pleasantries. This isn't a damn date or nothing. I lift one of Tease's smooth, creamy thighs up and out of the way with my hand, angling my cock to push inside of her. Her kisses get more fervent then, her fingernails cut into me harder, drawing blood and a slight brush of pain across my neck. *Kinky, bitch. I like it.* My stomach muscles tighten as I grab tight onto her ass cheek and pull her onto me, spearing her with my cock. Heat envelopes me and makes me shiver as I groan into the girl's mouth and start to pump my hips. Her body slams into the wall of the diner as I grunt and dig my way into that heat, balls tightening as I find myself slipping straight through all the cycles of pleasure straight down to a fuckin' orgasm. With a massive amount o' self control, I pull back, sliding mostly out of her, letting the air on my cock wake me up a slight smidge.

Tease opens her eyes and meets mine as I growl and shove myself fully inside of her, desperate for that wet heat around my cock. Her eyes widen a bit and her mouth parts fully, letting a whimper escape her lips that causes mine to curl. *Goddamn. Hot damn. Holy shit.*

"You are so fucking tight," I snarl because I can't fucking seem to control myself. The lack of sex, the fuck up today, all of that frustration is bleeding out of me and into her. And I don't give a shit. She's a prisoner of war right now, and while I'm tickled pink she wants to fuck me, I still don't fucking care what really happens to her. So I let my rage and my frustration boil up as I slam into her as hard as I can, knocking our pelvises together as her moans increase in pitch and her head falls back, lips trembling as she tries to speak. Can't get out a single word though, not one fucking word. "Like a virgin. Tight as a fucking virgin," I whisper into her ear, feeling her tightness wrap me harder, pulse quicker, like a pump, milking my cock for all it's worth. "A virgin fucking cock Tease." I bite at her ear and she screams, voice echoing strangely through all the open space around us. Her bare ass slaps a nice, earthy rhythm against the green siding of the building while the slick sound of our bodies moving together complements the song. *Amen.*

My hot breath mixes with hers, slides across her cheeks as I dig my fingers into her ass. She's getting so much tighter, I'm findin' it hard to move as fast, forcing my hips forward with each thrust so that I'm completely consumed by her pussy. If she isn't actually a virgin, then it's been awhile since she got some. I feel like I'm about to come again and prisoner or no, Beck does not disappoint the ladies. I reach my hand between us and find her breasts, sliding my hand down the cotton of the shirt and finding my way underneath. As soon as I find her bra, I tear it down, letting her full breasts spill over the top, teasing her pebbled nipples with rough fingers.

Tease's moans get louder, pressing against my neck, my jaw, my mouth. *Ah, ah, ah.* A chorus of whimpers that are increasing in pitch. *I got this baby in the bag.* I drop my hand down between us and find the hardened point of her clit, sliding two fingers around either side of it, pressing into her warm flesh gently but firmly. As soon as I start to move it around, chase her body into an even more fervent frenzy, the girl throws her head back and groans. Her pussy grabs hold of my cock, ridges grinding against my shaft while her wetness gives me the slickness I need to keep slidin'. Her fingers are scrambling at my back while her body starts to droop in my arms, relaxing into the frenzied fit of her climax.

When she raises her face back up and meets my gaze, mouth open wide, eyes even wider, I grit my teeth and give a few, last, good thrusts.

"Oh, hell yeah, baby," I groan as I slam Tease's ass into the wall a few last, desperate times, spilling my come inside of her. I keep rocking my body against her as the orgasm seizes me, finishing my load, shooting each and every last drop straight inside of her cunt. As soon as I finish, I'm ready to go again. There's not even a *second* of in-between time where I feel satisfied. I just want to keep fuckin'.

"Let go of me," she whispers, putting her hands on my chest. My fingers curl tightly around her ass as our juices mingle between her thighs, soaking my balls and getting me even hotter than I was before we started. "I'm done. Put me down." Tease stares me in the face with her green eyes. "Please, Beck."

The sound of my name from her lips convinces me to let go. I don't force myself on ladies; I only take what I'm being offered. With a grunt and a mournful groan, I slide my stiff cock out of her pussy and turn away, running my tongue over my lips. I'm so busy lookin' away and trying to sort out shit with my dick that I don't realize my mistake until too late.

Click.

There's a fuckin' gun to the back of my head.

Tease
CHAPTER 11

My hands are shaking but only from adrenaline. Only from that, right? I have to swallow three times and take massive breaths, filling my chest with air, expanding my lungs to full capacity so they can slow the rapid fire beat of my heart.

"Down on your fucking knees," I say, and I don't like the way my voice breaks a bit. *Wow.* Just oh my fucking God, wow. I didn't expect to enjoy that. I didn't *want* to enjoy that. I feel like an even bigger creep now than I did when I made the decision to go for it, to see if I could get Beck Evans to let his guard down.

"Now listen, sugar love, you don't want to head down this route." I take a small step back but keep the barrel aimed at the back of his skull, pointed straight at his thick, red hair. It felt so good curled around my fingertips, so soft, so smooth.

"Shut the fuck up!" The words burst from my throat in a

flurry. I'm so … confused right now. My body is shaking, my bare ass exposed to God knows how many people flying down that highway. What else did they all see? *My God, Tease.* Just standing here, with Beck's and my juices running down my inner thighs, teasing my legs with warmth, I feel like a traitor. To my club, to my brother, to myself. "I could hear the seriousness in your voice before. I knew you would shoot me dead if you had to. I hope you can hear it mine now, too." I take a deep breath, my jeans draped over my arm, swaying in the breeze. My hands are still shaking, and I feel light-headed. The fact that I don't hate what I just did, that I … liked it, makes me so mad I can't see straight. I had an orgasm. An actual, real live, fucking orgasm. Despite Beck's … praise, I'm not a virgin. But I've never gone all the way like that, felt my body exploding into a hundred thousand pieces. I was going to fake one, but I didn't have to. "Now down on your knees and give me your cellphone."

I take another step back as Beck drops to his knees with a growl, reaching his fingers into his pocket. I know he's got the hammer tucked in the back of his jeans still, but that's it. I checked. I almost forgot to. When my lips met his, fire took over my body and boiled my brain. The next few minutes were almost a blur. I had sex with Beck to distract him and ended up getting distracted myself.

"Now toss it back this way, nice and careful now." I watch him like a hawk, both hands wrapped around the gun, keeping my aim steady. I don't know how long I have. Somebody's bound to have heard us back here and might come snooping. I really, *really* want to put my pants back on.

"You're making a big mistake here, darling. Give me the gun back and we'll go inside, have some burgers and talk this shit out. Maybe give your brother a call and arrange something right here and now?" I ignore the smooth, sultry drawl of his voice as it wraps around my body and brings that wave of lust rushing back in full force. My nipples harden and my body pulses tight down below, drawing a slight groan from my throat. I swallow it away and shake my head, bending down carefully and staring at the cellphone. It's lying in the gravel next to my bare toes, but to grab it, I have to let go of the gun with one hand. *Damn it.* I ignore Beck's words and stay focused on his strong back, those rock hard muscles I felt beneath his shirt. He's a lot thicker than any guy I've ever been with, all hard bumps and valleys. The feel of all that power coiling beneath his skin was intoxicating. Or maybe I'm just attracted to him because he's forbidden, part of that foreign club I've been fantasizing about. That must be it.

I let go of the gun with my left hand, grabbing the phone carefully and standing up to retreat another step. I can still shoot him from far away, but he can't grab me. It just makes sense. I move my thumb across the screen.

It's password protected.

"What's the password?" I ask, hating how exposed I feel right now. I want my *damn* pants back on. Beck chuckles.

"Pussy lips," he says, and I wrinkle my nose. I'm used to

crudeness, grew up around it. But my brother doesn't like it. Whenever he catches language he doesn't appreciate, somebody ends up on dish duty, whether they're a prospect or a fully patched member. I've never once had to do it. I look at the back of Beck's head, grateful that I don't have to see his face. The sweat on his neck, his bright green eyes, his ruggedly beautiful features.

I try the password and it doesn't work.

"Capitals? A space?" I ask, and Beck laughs again, making me nervous. My whole life, I've been engrossed in the world of Seventy-seven Brothers and not once, *once*, has anything like this ever happened to me. My family's always protected me, kept me safe. I'm not used to this massive flow of adrenaline, this uncertainty. And I'm *definitely* not used to feeling the wind on my bare butt. "I am not fucking around here, Beck," I shout, getting more frustrated by the moment. I want to hate this man, but I can't. And that's pissing me off. Tears prick my eyes. "If anything's happened to my brother. If anything's happened to him … " I trail off and find my finger tensing on the trigger. When I imagine Darren lying lifeless on the side of the road somewhere, being lifted up and zipped into a body bag, my vision goes violet and I can't think straight.

"You gonna shoot me for giving you a false password?" My hand tenses up even further.

"I need to make a phone call." I don't know what else to say. I'm sure he can read me, and right now, I can't shoot him. He makes a move at me? And yeah, I could do it. If he told me my brother was dead ... but for a password? *So we're at a stalemate then?* This is like my life in a metaphor. A stalemate. The strange feelings that overwhelmed me on the porch peek their dirty heads up. *Triple M. You want to join the club, ride a bike, rob a bank. You want to be bad, don't you, Tease?* "And so do you. Why drag this out? You don't need to cart me all the way to Nashville. Give me the password and I'll let you go, let you walk right out of here, climb on your bike, and ride away."

"All I want is my fucking friend back. She's had a hard life; she don't need this shit. I let you go, I lose my chance at ever seeing her again."

"Let me go? I'm not the hostage anymore, Beck. You are."

"You positive on that one, lemon cake?" I swallow hard and then all of a sudden, he's moving, springing to his feet in a coil of muscles and power. I fire the gun, but the bullet whizzes right past him, exploding into the side of a minivan. The window shatters as I pull my finger down on the trigger again and get ... nothing. There's only one bullet in the fucking gun.

Beck appears in my face, grabbing my wrists and hauling me against his chest. I manage to keep hold of the weapon this time, but it doesn't do me any good. I might as well be wearing steel shackles. Beck Evans doesn't just have vanity muscles. I feel like he could crush the bones in my arms with his fingers if he so wanted to.

"Military?" I whisper because I've never seen anyone but

Oren move like this. I know he served a stint in the U.S. Army when he was younger. I don't wish and pray and hope that he made it out okay. I feel terrible because Oren is family, and I would die for him if I had to, but ... whatever happened, happened right? I know he wants me as his old lady. It's just a matter of time before he gets the nerves to announce that to my brother.

"How ever did you guess?" Beck murmurs, sliding his fingers down my arm and pulling the gun away. I notice that his eyes travel down between us, towards the stiff bulge in his pants. I sniff and raise my chin up, trying to be strong, trying to get through this as best I can. Beck's green eyes snap right back up to mine, two emerald orbs shimmering with false amusement. He was hurting earlier, and there's no way all of that pain and worry disappeared. It's a good front, but I see straight through it.

"What are you going to do to me now?" I ask, swallowing hard. Beck shakes his head and looks around, tucking his gun under his shirt about a half-second before heads appear around the side of the diner. *Shit.* I scramble to pull my jeans back on and Beck lets me, raising his hand to the curious faces of folks with cellphones clutched in their fingers.

"Lovers' quarrel, ladies and gentleman. Nothing to see here." I button up my jeans and force myself to breathe through my nose. Beck slides his arm around my waist and I close my eyes tight. "Relax, Tease. I told you, I'm not going to hurt you. That's not my goal here. You play nice; I play nice." He kisses my ear, and unwanted shivers crawl across my skin. *Did I open up a can of worms by having sex with him? What if he forces himself on me?* I open my eyes up. I'll do what I have to do here, no matter what.

I glance over at Beck and then at the mutilated minivan.

"Damn near sure we've worn out our welcome here. Hop on the bike, babe, and let's go. We'll find somewhere else to eat." Beck motions for me to move ahead of him, and I hesitate, watching the people around us, weighing my options. I don't know what the club did back there, and even though I don't believe Beck's story about a rooftop gunman, I can't get the police involved. If I run to one of these people and beg for their help, that's what's going to happen.

I nod my head and start walking, pausing only to bend down and grab my jacket, feet sore on the rough gravel of the parking lot. Beck moves along behind me, shadowing me but not touching. When we get to his bike and climb on, his warm body nestled against mine, feelings roar up deep inside of me. Feelings that I clamp down on, push back and ignore.

I'm good at that. I've always been good at that.

Maybe that's my problem?

Tease
CHAPTER 12

The rumble of the road and the press of Beck's body makes me want to go to sleep, to nap right there in his arms with the wind blasting my face and yanking my red hair back. *Such a traitor*, I think to myself. And not just to the club, but also to me, personally. I am *not* as bothered by being kidnapped as I should be. I was willing to wager my body to get the advantage here, and now? I've become complacent. I don't focus on the throb of heat between my legs, the wetness that persists even now. That's the last thing I need to worry about. I'll deal with that later, with the fact that we didn't use a condom and any number of things that could mean.

Another hour down the road, with the sun nearing its descent in the sky, we stop at another restaurant. Beck climbs off before me and has his cell immediately in hand, waiting with bated breath for an answer. I examine him in the harsh white wash of the parking lot lights. He's managed to wipe most of the blood away, but his red T-shirt is crusted with it underneath his leather vest. I don't know how he expects to walk into the restaurant without anybody taking notice of either him or me. I am now the girl with no shoes on.

A smile tweaks my face.

Who's watching me, I wonder? Who's looking at me and wondering where I've been, why I look the way I look?

I continue to watch Beck, using my people-watching skills to take in all his details. There's a fine brush of red stubble across his chin, enough to give him a rough, unpolished look that's at odds with the constant smile on his sensual mouth. Those green eyes, so like mine, but yet so different. The color is remarkably similar, but Beck has the weight of experience in his gaze. I'm sure mine is sheltered and unremarkable, but jaded, too. I think I'm fairly unique in that aspect. A girl who grew up in a motorcycle club, saw things she shouldn't see, heard things she never wanted to hear, but who was also kept. I'm kept, a kept woman.

My eyes trail down Beck's neck, to his wide chest, his round shoulders and the rolling curve of bicep that emerges from his shirt sleeves. His arms are covered in tattoos, all black and gray, mostly reapers and skulls. There are a few words scattered here and there, an eagle. But that's about all I can make out. I keep my examination moving downwards, over his fingers, and I get horribly vivid flashbacks of his hand cupping my ass, his cock spreading me wide and slipping deep inside.

I turn away abruptly, my body melting into itself, convincing me that I need another bite of Beck Evans. If it comes down to it, and I think I can take advantage of him again, I will. If he ever lets his guard down again. Hopefully this will be over before I get the chance to find out. I'm a bit worried about spending the night with him. At this point, it might not come down to my finding an advantage to sleep with him. He could just take me. It happens more than you'd want to think in this world. I wrap my arms around myself, touching my fingers to the dusty jacket. I imagine that he might ask me to take it off again and my nails dig into my arms painfully.

"Oh, thank the fucking stars! You son of a bitch," Beck whoops, lifting a hand up towards the sky. But his eyes keep finding mine, always watching. He must've been a real asset to the military. So how did he end up here, in this life? I was born into it, so I don't get the whole choosing part. Who simply decides, *I'm going to join a motorcycle gang*? The things our prospects have to suffer through, the girls who come looking for a place to belong, they go through initiation periods that are virtual hells. And there's no guarantees either. Some women hang around the clubhouse, work for us, bring in money, clean, and they never get claimed as old ladies. Never. "Where you at?" Beck listens for a moment, touching his hand to his chin. His face shifts, almost imperceptibly, before he takes up a flat smile again. "No shit." The words are spoken so quietly, I almost miss them. "That many, huh?" Another pause. "Yeah, I got the girl."

I raise my chin and wait to see what he says. Tax would walk through fire to get me back, so that's not the issue. Provided he's still around. If he's not … then it isn't just the sorrow and pain of losing my brother that's going to bite me in the ass, it'll be a hell of a lot worse. The house is in his name; the club serves in his name. If Tax is gone, I'll become one of those ladies I've always pitied, searching for someone to claim me as their own. I wait with bated breath.

"Alright, Pres. You're the damn boss." Beck pulls a pack of cigarettes out of his pocket and offers me one. I take it tentatively and wait while he gets out a lighter. "Roger that." He listens in for another minute and then closes his eyes real slow. "We'll figure it out, Austin. We always do." And then Beck hangs up, weighing his cell in his hand for a moment as he smokes the cigarette. I take a drag, too, holding the smoke in my lungs for as long as I can. I exhale only when Beck looks up at me. "Can't expect you to walk in there with no fuckin' shoes on, now can I?" he asks, slipping the phone away and going to his saddlebags. Beck digs around for a moment and emerges with a pair of pink flip flops, topped off with a purple flower. They're not my style, not his either I would imagine. "A lady friend of mine left these behind. I snagged them, just waitin' for a situation like this to come along." He tosses them to me as I swing my leg over the bike and stand up.

"A situation like this? In which you kidnap a girl? Use

her as a bartering chip against a rival MC?" Beck grins and pulls his cigarette out from between his lips. His smile gets a little wider.

"A situation where I got a lady missin' her shoes. Happens more often than you might think. Sometimes, when you're bangin' on the fly, shit happens. Angry husbands or boyfriends or what not. Occasionally a quick getaway is in order for both of us." Beck tosses his smoke to the ground and crushes it into the pavement. "Now, are you going to behave yourself, walk in there and have a Coke with me? Or are we going to play around again?"

I smile back at him.

"It's cold out tonight."

Beck laughs raucously, tossing his head back.

"Shoot, it's warmer than a whore's cunt out here."

"I want my jacket, please." I touch my fingers to the leather, pursing my lips and waiting while he looks me over, eyes cutting deeper than I'd like them to. "This area, it's not home to any club. Nobody will even notice the patches on our jackets, I promise you that. I have a lot of free time on my hands, and Seventy-seven Brothers is my life. We're very careful not to step on anyone else's toes. Something that you and yours could learn something about." Beck laughs at me again. Everything is fucking funny to this man.

I take a step back and bump into the warm metal of his Suzuki Savage as Beck leans forward, getting so close to me that I have to look up to keep hold of his gaze. Our foreheads touch, just enough that I can feel the sweat on his skin.

"You've got balls, Miss Emilie 'Tease' Hathorne. Wear your damn coat, but don't cause me any trouble. Your President knows we got you, and you're right: he wants your ass back real, real bad. We're arranging a meeting place as soon as Melissa can be moved." Beck looks off to the side for a second, like he's trying to process the thought.

"I told you, Seventy-seven Brothers is a family. And we understand family. If they have your friend, they'll keep her alive. That's what we do. We don't post armed gunmen on roofs." I blink and my eyelashes actually brush across Beck's skin. His turn to shiver as he pulls back and looks me up and down again. In his pants, I can see the shadow of his cock, hard and ready. My palms start to sweat and I get nervous again.

"Then who did, Tease? Who shot my friend in the back?"

"If my brother ordered that, she wouldn't have been hit in the back; she'd be dead."

Beck stares at me, gaze hard, like he's trying to determine whether or not I'm lying to him. I keep my eyes open and my face still. After a moment, he pulls away, shaking his head.

"We lost ten people today, Tease. Ten. One in five of the people I called family are dead." Beck turns to look at me. "Eight of yours. So, eighteen people died because someone fired that shot. Now, who the fuck would do that?"

"Eighteen?" I ask, mouth dry. Beck ignores the question

and starts off towards the doors to the restaurant. I grew up with this club; I know everybody. Everybody. Everybody. But at least my brother's okay, right? He said the President. "Tax," I say, slipping my feet into the flip flops and following after Beck. I completely dismiss any fantasies of hitting him in the back of the head or anything like that. This man obviously knows his shit. Getting the jump on him is going to take something big, like sex. But even that was just barely. I may just decide to wait this out. "The President. You said President. Is it Tax?"

"Ain't nobody being real specific here. This is all a bit of a clusterfuck. We're all a little scatterbrained at the moment. In short, I don't rightly know."

I fight tears, pushing them back for another day. I won't show this man any emotion. *Eight people dead*? I run my hands down my cheeks, blinking hard as we enter into the bright light of the restaurant. Beck holds the door open for me as I shuffle inside in my borrowed shoes. I refuse to think about where they came from.

"Table for two there, twinkle toes," Beck says to the waiter. I watch as he pulls the wool over his own eyes, hiding from the emotion I saw in him this morning when he snatched me off my porch. I bet there's a lot of that buried deep down inside. I … felt it when we were having sex, too. Beck is a bottle whose top is about to burst off.

I follow him to the table and scoot into the seat opposite the green-eyed devil. It feels so wrong to sit here with a menu, under these fluorescent lights and pretend like everything is normal, like I'm out on a cheap date. I purse my lips tight.

"Don't need these plastic sheets there, friend," Beck says, grabbing my menu from my fingers and tossing them both to the end of the table. The waiter sets our water glasses down and stands there looking like he'd rather be anywhere but here. "Two burgers, medium, with fries. Two Cokes. Make it quick. I am fuckin' starved." The man grabs our menus and retreats with a small exhalation of breath.

Awkward silence descends around us. Or maybe it just descends around me. Beck doesn't seem to acknowledge it. He sits there staring at my face, tapping his fingers on the speckled gray laminate of the tabletop. The word *less* stares back at me from his knuckles. *I can't believe I had sex with this man.* I think this, but even as I do, I know it's a bit of a lie. I can smell his spicy, warm scent from across the table. My eyes unconsciously trace the lines on his arms, sorting through the darkness of his tattoos and focusing on the bronzed skin beneath. My throat gets a little tighter.

"When are we meeting for the exchange?" I ask, acting as if this is any other business transaction. The right side of Beck's lip twitches up into a smile. He rubs at the blood stains on his shirt, the ones that actually aren't drawing as many suspicious glances as I thought. The people in this diner are all quiet, bent over coffee. Mostly truckers, I guess. They probably don't give a fuck about some biker in a bloody shirt. I bet they see a lot worse.

"A week."

I almost explode from my seat.

"A week?" I ask, curling my hands around the edge of the table. My heart speeds up again, but I ignore it, mostly because I'm afraid of what it might mean. *Triple M.* I get to meet the other people, get to see how they work from the inside. This also means I'm stuck with Beck. I cross an arm over my chest and grab onto my bicep, digging my nails into the gray cotton of my shirt. A lot can happen in a week. "I have to go an entire week without knowing who I've lost?"

"You play nice; I play nice," Beck repeats, drawing my temper out again. I don't mean to get so riled up, but something shifted in me after we had sex. I just feel angry with him. I can't fucking explain it.

"Yeah, well, you keep saying that, but what does that mean?" I don't bother to keep my voice down. It's obvious now that nobody cares what we're doing here. We're in the middle of Goddamn nowhere right now. "You want me to be your whore for the week? Give you favors in exchange for favors?"

"You been hangin' out with the wrong crowd, sugar tits."

"I don't like pet names," I tell him honestly. I especially hate the term *princess.* Beck raises his red brows and leans forward. His face is so rough and handsome, so masculine. Even his mouth, full and sensual, doesn't have a drop of femininity. Beck is a man's man if I've ever seen one, and trust me – I've seen a lot. He's older than me, not excessively so, but there's definitely an age gap here. Beck has very thin, very fine laugh lines at the edges of his eyes. Instead of seeing it as a flaw, I find it hot. I don't know why. Obviously this man isn't as simple and carefree as he pretends to be. Still, nobody with lines like that can ever be considered austere or straitlaced, not like my brother at all.

"Your fuckin' nickname is Tease, and you don't like pet names? You tell me how the hell that makes any good sense." Beck sits back and slaps his palms on the table.

"As far as you're concerned, my *real* name is Tease. That's what I go by. It's not a pet name; it's a fact of my life. I hang out at the clubhouse and I look good because that's what everybody expects from me. It's the easiest way for me to keep my brother out of hot water with the rest of the guys. I'm a drain on the group, and I don't put out, and I don't work, so I have to do fucking something, okay?" I get angrier than I mean to, leaning forward and then slumping back. "I am a cock tease. A tease. Tease. That's my fucking name."

"Your fucking name is *Emilie*. Wear what your momma gave you with pride." Beck and I stare at each other with our green gazes, speaking the same language in different dialects. "How the fuck old are you anyhow? A little young to be so cynical, don't you think?"

"I'm eighteen." Beck whistles under his breath, shaking his head and running his fingers through his hair. I stare at the patches on the front of his vest and pretend his reaction isn't bothering me.

"Woo wee. Shit, fuck and damn. You are young. I hate being right sometimes." Beck looks around and then gets out a cigarette. Nobody seems to care when he lights up. "You don't sound like any eighteen year old I ever met. What's the matter with you, woman? Where's your sense of fun?" I tilt my head to the side and stare at him.

"Fun? What fun am I supposed to be having here, with you? You kidnapped me. You took my family members away from me." I touch a hand to my chest and fight the tears back. I almost don't want to know who's gone. If I don't know, it can't hurt me. I swallow hard and sink into the red pleather of the bench seat.

Beck doesn't answer for awhile, smoking his cigarette and staring out the window at the darkened sky. Stars are twinkling like diamonds, wrapped in a sea of black velvet. The diner is quiet, just a slight clinking of silverware and the gentle clatter of porcelain in the background.

"I don't act eighteen because I don't feel eighteen. I've had a strange life. My father and my brother were very protective of me and my sister." *Fuck, Tease, why are you telling this man your life story? He doesn't care. And even if he did, he doesn't have a right to know.* I think of Lizzie, living in her apartment near the college, going to school for engineering. She's basically the opposite of me. A wild party girl with an independent streak. She's always known what she wanted, and when the time came, she went out and took it. I bet she'd like Beck. "What about you? You act like a teenage boy. What's your story? How old are you?" I try not to sound too eager, but I'm kind of desperate to know. I've only been with ... boys before. I had sex with two of my high school boyfriends, and only a handful of times. I've never been with a real man. I slide my hand down my arm and feel goose bumps. In the back of my mind, I keep trying to tell myself it doesn't count because I did it for reasons other than lust or love. But I know it really does, maybe even more than any other encounter I've ever had with a guy.

"I'm dumb as a bag o' hammers, and I ain't got no sense. Life's more enjoyable that way, you know?" Beck winks at me, and his smile turns into a sizzling smirk. I can tell he knows what I'm thinking. "And shoot, I'm an ol' man. Why do you want to know my age?" I cross my arms over my chest and glance up as the waiter appears and delivers our Cokes, no straws, no smile. Guess he doesn't like Beck's pet names either.

I watch as Beck drags his drink over and downs near half of it in one gulp. I like the way his throat muscles move as he swallows, the slight swell of his Adam's apple bobbing slightly. I wrap my fingers around my sweating glass and wait for him to finish.

"Ah, that hit the fucking spot," he growls, making my body purr in response. I look away and bite my lip hard to get control of myself. This is fucking stupid. So fucking stupid. Now I *am* acting like a horny eighteen year old. "You done talkin' to me, sweets?"

"I might be," I whisper, taking hold of the mixed bag of emotions I've got hanging around in my gut. I wrap them up and toss the out the window, looking for that calm, apathetic disconnect I'm so good at. It's like that weird calmness Beck pulls over himself. We are pretty similar in a lot of ways.

"How 'bout this? I'm thirty years old, and all I have in my life worth living for are my friends." I look back at him and see that he's still smiling, but with a heavy melancholy in his gaze. "You and I, we ain't so different. I'm sorry about what happened today, I really am. But maybe we can call a truce for now?" He lets his smile melt into a grin. *Defense mechanism.* But that's okay – we all need one occasionally. "After all, I had a real good time earlier today."

I breathe in deep and try to find the right words to say, but nothing'll come out. I open my lips and close them tight. Shit. He knows now. I don't think he did at first, but he does now.

"And good job on that one. I didn't see it comin'. You almost got me there, sugar, and that rarely fuckin' happens." Beck finishes his cigarette and pushes open the window next to him, flicking it out into the night. "And," Beck leans forward on his elbows, ignoring the waiter when he sets our meals down in front of us. "If you ever want to try again, I'm more than willing." I reach out for my plate, looking him in the face and nearly exploding from my skin when he clasps his warm, sweaty hand around mine. My heart jumps into my throat as I struggle to breathe. "But if you don't, I won't touch you. You can bet your tits on that."

Beck lets go of me and sits back, spinning his plate of food around and throwing me a smile.

C.M. Stunich

A moment later, I smile back.

CHAPTER 13

Austin doesn't want me to come all the way to Nashville. I don't tell Tease, but her President, her brother I guess, doesn't just want her back. He is fucking furious, not just about the kidnapping but also the fight that went down. So am I, but fuck and shit? Who the hell fired their gun on Melissa? If that wasn't a call to arms, what was? I'm mourning, too; I'm grieving, too. Doesn't matter to Seventy-seven Brothers though. They want us to take responsibility for what happened back there, admit to starting the fight, and then they want a whole other host of shit that ain't ever going to happen.

I zip down the interstate looking for a place to stay. My pick is going to be random, somewhere off the beaten path and out of sight. I gotta keep our trump card secret. Emilie Hathorne. *Shoot.* She is tough shit and a whole handful of hotness. I still can't believe she was able to pull my gun on me *and* fire a shot. I guess I was mesmerized by that tight, young pussy of hers. *Fuck.* That is exactly what she wanted, and I fell right into the trap. I might just feel a bit slighted that she didn't want me for me, you know what I'm sayin'. I'm a good lookin' guy, right? This is by far the most lady trouble I have had in a good, long while.

Oh well. Miss Tease here and I are going to be hanging out until we can sort this shit out. We hand her back now and then what we will have? Melissa, yes, but probably not for long. Last thing Triple M needs right now is a full on war with an MC as organized and well run as Seventy-seven Brothers. They will flat out fucking destroy us.

I don't let my brain dwell on the lives lost today. That'll come later, in the night no doubt. Sometime in the future, I am going to wake up screamin'. But at least I know the people I'm closest to are alright: Austin, Gaine, Mireya, and Kimmi. And Melissa Diamond. She is actually a-fucking-live. I don't know why Seventy-seven Brothers decided they were going to snatch her up, but it's a blessing. They coulda just shot her dead.

I swing down an exit, enjoying the feel of Tease's hair against my neck. I got a helmet strapped to the back of my ride, but I haven't given it to her to wear. I like being able to smell her sweetness, the gentle allure of shampoo. My dick has been perpetually hard since we fucked earlier. I didn't get any release from that shit, and I'm ready for a second round. Tease, though, I'm having a hard time figuring her out. I don't know if she wants me or not.

Get through this, Beck. This is a low point in life, but that's alright. 'S all about balance. I got shit, so next round, I'm gettin' gold.

I swing into a parking lot and slide up to the front doors of the lobby. Tease doesn't look all that excited about our stop, but that's alright. Soon as this is over, she can go back to her clubhouse and her MC.

"Come on in and let's get ourselves a room. I am damn near beat." I hold out my hand for Tease's, but she doesn't take it, climbing off my metal beauty with grace and a confident half-smile on her face. I have no clue what she's thinkin', but at least she's cooperating right now. I like the girl, but I have to be careful with her. If she somehow managed to get a hold of her brother and told him how to find us, I would be fucked up ass creek without any lube. Yee-fucking-Haw. That would be some major hurting and then probably end up with me pushin' up Goddamn daisies.

I make Tease walk in front of me, guiding her up to the counter with my hand on her lower back. I got plenty o' money on me, thanks to Austin and Kimmi's latest conquest. Good thing about dealing with motels like this is, they take cold, hard cash and don't ask questions. We're not staying at no fancy bed and breakfast like we were in Korbin, but that's alright. I ain't picky.

"Room 105," I say, tucking our keycard in my front pocket and moving back out to my bike to grab my stuff. Tease doesn't say a word to me until we actually get in the room, and I start first thing with unplugging the phone from the wall. I open the sliding glass doors that lead out to the pool area and toss the damn thing in the bushes nearby. It'll be there when we check out, and this keeps Tease from getting easy access to it.

"I won't pretend I have any clue what you're doing," Tease says, leaning against the wall with her eyes locked on me. She's stopped looking for petty routes of escape. By now she'll have recognized that I am a genuine badass extraordinaire. I chuckle at my own inner joke and squeeze past her, leaving the sliding glass doors unlocked. If she tries to run, I can catch her pretty easy. I still got some skills left over from my time wearing a green beret.

"Give you a hint. It has to do with the bed and a pair of handcuffs." Tease raises her brows and gives me an odd look. I put my hands on my hips and stare right back at her, taking in the ugly orange linens on the single bed, the faded paintings, the crooked desk, all out of the corner of my eye. "I gotta get some sleep, too. Since I'm on duty by myself, I have to take precautions. Hope you don't mind, but you'll be sleeping in cuffs tonight. I'll try to make it pleasant for ya."

I breathe out, letting go of the day along with it. Picking up a lady tonight isn't an option, and I've been riding all day, so my priority right now is finding some way to relax. I need to let some pressure out of the cooker, or I'm goin' to blow my top. I move past Tease, tasting her scent on my tongue as I slide open the doors and step out onto the pavement. Surprisingly, she follows along with me. Thank

Christ because I don't know what I'd do if I was dealing with someone like Mireya, all headstrong and full of claws. To kidnap her, I'd have to keep her perpetually knocked out and dreamin'. On the other hand, Tease isn't screamin' and cryin' neither. We both know what's going on here, what's at stake for both of us. It's just easier to go along with the flow.

The air tonight is a little wet, hinting at a storm somewhere far off. I let the electricity of it swirl around me as I move across the pavement and pause underneath a row of palm trees. Just beyond a black metal fence, there's a pool and a flippin' hot tub.

I smile.

Amen, Mother Mary. There's how I'm going to be spending my evening. I glance over at Tease.

"You up for a dip?" I ask her, and she crinkles her brows at me. The wind picks up her ruby red hair and swirls it around in front of her face and across her neck. I watch as she pulls it back and licks her lips. Most of the red lipstick she was wearing earlier has worn off, giving her a more natural look. I'm not sure which I like better. Guess all the faces of this woman are beautiful.

"I'm a little lacking in the clothing department, so I think I'll pass." I shrug and move back to the room, sliding the doors closed and making sure they're locked before I head inside the fence and over to the hot tub. It's dark out, most of the lights in the surrounding rooms are off. I take it the pool area's probably closed at this time, but fuck 'em. What are they gonna do? Ask me to leave?

I laugh again and slip off my vest, laying it gently across a nearby chair before I strip off my shirt. The evening air teases my skin and hardens my nipples into points. I can *feel* the power of the sky right here, and it is *hot*. Or maybe I'm just feelin' Tease's eyes on my body, raking over the muscles in my midsection, sliding up to the Jolly Roger tattoo across my chest. I flash her a wink as she sits down on another chair and leans back, pretending not to care that I'm half-naked. I lick my lips and touch a hand to my belly, enjoying the way her bright eyes follow mine. She doesn't have a damn ass clue how fucking hot she looks draped over that chair, red hair framing her pale face.

"You're not going to run off on me, are you?" I ask.

"Let me guess, you'll catch me if I do?"

I move over to her, watching the way her body contracts, the muscles in her arms and face tightening as I come in close, bending over and grabbing onto the arm rests on either side of her body. But I don't touch her. A promise is a promise, even in this fucked up world we all live in.

"You want to find out? I'd love to chase after your ass."

"We're not friends, Beck Evans," she tells me, turning on her side and facing towards the bubbling waters of the spa. I step back and reach down for the button on my jeans, flicking it open and sliding the zipper down nice and slow. Almost immediately Tease's gaze comes back to me, pupils dilating as she watches me drop my jeans to the ground, kicking my boots off and climbing into that water butt friggin' naked.

I don't try to hide my hard-on. What's the Goddamn point? I think you could see this baby from space.

"Oh, fuck, yes," I groan as the scalding water envelopes my body, gliding over my erection and soaking me straight up to my pecs. I sit on the cement bench facing Tease, noticing the fluttery pulse in her throat, the tightness of her hands. My fists clench at my sides as I try to relax back into the jets and let come what may. I am fucking horny though, like a damn bull in heat. If I had my way tonight, Miss Hathorne would be joining me in here, straddling my lap and riding me like a fuckin' horse. "Nice and warm and wet in here if you want to join me."

"You definitely go about kidnappings in a strange way, Beck," Tease tells me, sounding a little more like an eighteen year old girl and less like an old lady. I feel a little guilty about her age, but damn if she isn't a woman. Those curves, that ass, her sweet thighs. I could spend all day fantasizing about that moment. Sex that hot only comes along once in a great while. "If I get in there, I'm wearing my shirt at least, but then what happens when I get out? Do you have any women's clothing stuffed in your saddlebags?"

"You ain't gonna skinny dip with me?" I stand up and let the water slide off my abs, letting the dim lighting around the pool reflect off of the wetness and turn the tables on Miss Tease. So she's used to getting guys all hot and bothered? I wonder how well she'll take it when the tables are turned. I spin around and examine the mostly dark rooms. Those that are lit all have the curtains pulled closed. "Ain't nobody looking right now, sweetheart." I finish my sweep and catch her gaze again. Her pupils have taken up most of the green in her eye, giving her a hungry look that sets my nerves on fire. *I fucking want you so hard it hurts*, I think to myself, holding back a small growl.

"What happens if I do?" she asks, and I love the way her voice drops an octave, like she doesn't even know she's doin' it. Her accent turns me on, too. It's a slightly less country version o' mine, more refined, not as crude. I shrug my shoulders and give her another grin, settling back into the water with a sigh and a groan.

"That's up to the laws of this great and vast universe. I guess we'll have to take it slow and find out." Tease sits up and looks around for a moment before rising to her feet and shedding her leather jacket. *Fuck yeah, darlin'. Take it off.*

"I'll dip my feet in, how's that?" she asks, setting the coat down and moving over to the edge. I watch in disappointment as she settles down on the cement and starts to roll up the legs of her jeans. "And then we can talk and maybe you could consider letting me call my brother?"

"Now why in the blasted depths of hell would I do that? Arrangements have already been made. You lost out on your chance back at the first diner." I lean back and lay my arms on the cement, closing my eyes against the stress of the day. I knew it was comin', I did. But I just didn't expect the consequences. Ten fucking people are dead? Ten. And we didn't lose a damn one in the last shoot out. I blame myself for it. I'm the one responsible for keepin' us alive. I open my eyes again and focus on Tease. Last thing I want right now are those ten names running through my mind over and over again. Austin already had the weight o' guilt hanging on his words. I have to stay strong or we'll never survive as a club.

"All I want to do is make sure he's alright, find out who I've lost." Tease leans towards me, her face catching the steam from the roiling water. "Don't I have a right to know that?"

"Might be best you *don't* know. At least for the time being. Ignorance really is bliss." I watch her fingers clamp down on the pavement, nails scraping as she struggles to control a flurry of emotions. I feel bad for the girl, I do, but I'd do it all over again. Taking her was the only way to ensure our survival, to ensure Melissa's. "Now quit pussyfooting around and get your ass in here." She actually glares at me then, but I'm not trying to be an asshole. I know I come across as one most of the time anyhow, but I'm actually tryin' to help. I pull my arms back into the water and rub at my chin with wet fingers. "Listen, I know we ain't had the best day today. I get that. But you know what else I know? That life isn't always perfect. The good and the bad, they come in waves. We can't prepare for every horrible thing coming our way, not even when we're trying our damnedest, so I'll tell you something. Pay real close attention here because this is hard-earned honesty." Tease lifts her chin up and sits ramrod straight, but at least she stops glaring at me. "Take every moment, every fuckin' *second*, that you can to enjoy life. Don't live in years or months or even weeks. Don't live for tomorrow or someday, live for right fucking now. You mighta heard this a hundred times, but it always bears repeating. You never know when the moment you're living is going to be your last, so enjoy it." I hold up my hand and gesture at the water around me. "Sit in this fucking hot tub with me and relax, look at the stars, take a breath. I can guarantee you if you do that even were you to die five minutes from now, you wouldn't regret it. Tease, those folks, our friends and family, those people we lost today, they didn't know they were goin' down in a hail of gunfire. But I'll tell you what I do know, that the ones who spent that morning lounging on the beach, they didn't feel slighted."

I sit back and run my wet hand through my hair. *Christ, that was a big speech, even for a loudmouth like me.* I'm not entirely sure where the damn thing came from, but if this girl can walk out of here havin' learned something from me, I'll be a better man for it.

"Did you learn that in the military?" she asks me, looking around the deserted pool area, at the discarded white towels draped across lounge chairs, the spots of water staining the ground around us.

"Shoot, sugar, I learned that in life." I stare at her and wonder how she ended up the way she is. She's jaded, but she's also naïve. Ain't never seen a woman like this, 'specially not an ol' lady. What a strange life she must lead.

After a second of silence, Tease digs her fingers under her shirt and tosses it towards my discarded pile of clothes. Her black bra teases me mercilessly with its lacy cups, framing the perfect, pale line of her cleavage like a picture frame. I have to tense my fingers on the bench to stay still. The pressure of the water and the jets is near enough to make me blow my load right here, right now. I look away and chuckle under my breath. A splash of water follows and when I glance back, the girl's in the spa still dressed in her jeans.

"I'm not wearing underwear," is her response. I think it's meant to be an explanation, but instead it comes across as an invitation.

"Oh, I remember well," I say, looking at her looking back at me. I know somewhere, way back, my family's got some Irish blood. At this point, I'd just consider myself Southern and be done with it, but it's pretty obvious that Tease and I got some things in common. Red hair, green eyes, skin that's pale underneath my perpetual fuckin' tan. I don't usually go for girls like this. My type's more leggy and blonde, but hot damn if I'm not sittin' here grinding my teeth and fighting an attraction that makes less sense than tits on a bull. "And if you were so inclined to take those fuckers off, I swear on my momma's grave that I wouldn't be lookin'." I pause and my voice slips out in a deep growl. "Not unless you wanted me to."

"Well, I don't," Tease says, but she don't sound all that convinced. I keep my attention focused on the blue and white tiles that line the wall, trying my damnedest to dredge up come self-fucking-control. What a name though, *Tease*. I can see where she gets it now. I can only imagine what it would be like to walk around lookin' at her beauty, her curves, her silky hair, day in and day out. Bound to drive a man to his grave. "I'm not even sure I should be talking to you, sitting here like this. The fact that I'm even doing this, that I'm not fighting to the death, that makes me a traitor. I should've let you shoot me. Now, I'm a liability to the club and to my family."

I snap my gaze back to her face, but she's not crying, not even frowning.

"'That's ridiculous. Ain't nobody would wish their family dead over some stupid shit as that. Hell, I should've told Austin to take the hit, dropped our jackets and left. If I'd have known it was going to be a life or death, thing, I'd have chosen life. Pride is great and all that, but it don't mean shit when you're six feet under and rotting."

"Not everybody in this world would agree with you," Tease tells me, standing up like she's planning on getting out. I smile at her, but it's not an entirely pleasant look.

"Well then they haven't seen the things I've seen. I've spent my life on the right side of the fence and the wrong. I served in the U.S Army Special Forces and as a one-percenter, racking up all the wrong kind of karma in a club I can hardly believe I ever got out of." I watch her hesitation as she stands there, her soggy jeans threatening to slip over her hips. "So, I don't care what you think. You ain't no traitor."

Tease swallows and brushes her hair behind one ear. The tips are wet and clinging to her mostly bare chest, drawing my attention right back to her breasts. She doesn't have massive tits, but they're perky as hell. I can still feel 'em against my fingertips, and I doubt it's a memory I'm going to soon forget. I'm not a big believer in fate, but it almost feels like the fuckin' stars above aligned, so I could meet this girl. Don't know why I think that. Kind of a stupid fucking thought considering folks had to die for it, but everything comes at a price, don't it?

"Those aren't the only reasons I'm a traitor," she says to me, her voice soft but firm. I watch as she bites her lip and struggles with something inside. When that gaze finally turns to me, framed in dark lashes that curl up towards her porcelain skin, I am almost fucking done for. My nostrils flare and my muscles tense as I struggle to stay seated. Doesn't help when she wades over to me and reaches out with questing fingertips. Tease stops short of actually touching the Triple M tattoo on my shoulder but she comes real, real close to it. "I'm a traitor because I should be trying to kill you when instead I'm sitting here trying not to be attracted to you." Tease closes that gap between her fingers and my shoulder, turning the burn in my stomach to a roaring flame.

I reach out and grab onto her hips, yanking her towards me until Tease is straddling me in her wet jeans, sliding her body along my swollen cock. The feel of the denim grating against my skin is painful pleasure, drawing a groan from my mouth as we lock lips. She raises her hands and presses them against my chest, drawing back for an agonizing breath. When she opens her mouth to speak, I cut her off with another kiss. Live in the moment. That's what we're going to fucking do. I hope that was her intention because I don't know if I'm going to be able to stop now.

Her fingers touch my pecs, curling tight, exploring my skin as I roam across hers. I rock my hips up against her sweet spot, cursing those damn Levi's so hard I could make God blush. I want 'em *off*. Tease moves with me, gyrating her hips and grinding her body into my erection, giving it to me without giving it up.

"Tease," I snarl against her mouth, my teeth scrapin' up against her lower lip. Water rushes around and between us, soothing heat against our aching bodies. "You are such a fucking tease." I chuckle at my own joke, kissing my way across her jaw and down her neck, over to her shoulder and flickin' my tongue across the single rose tattoo on her upper arm.

"I can't do this. I want to stop doing this," she groans as my hands find the clasp on her bra and set those babies free. "I cannot fucking do this."

"Live in the moment, Emilie," I groan, jerking her forward and crushing her breasts against my chest. At the mention of her name, she gets all buck wild on me and grabs my face between her hands. Her mouth works at mine furiously, like she can't get enough. I cup her ass with my hands and keep grinding, slamming my dick against her jeans until the pressure's too much and I come, spilling my junk into the frothing waters of the spa. *I feel real, real bad for the next people who climb on in here.*

"I'm a bad person," Tease groans as I push her back, my body furious at the lack of release. I came, but I ain't done. I need more or I'm goin' to have some seriously blue balls come tomorrow. "I didn't put out for anyone in the club, and now I'm going all the way for you." I pause as I look down at her, rising to my feet and cupping her under the chin.

"It's your body, sugar lips. You decide when and where and how."

"But right now, I – " I cut her off with another kiss, pushing the soggy jeans into the hot tub and using my foot to get them off her ankles. They're at least a couple sizes too big – fortunately for me. You ever try to strip those skinny jean things off a chick? Hot damn. It's like puttin' the pussy under lock and denim key.

"Besides," I whisper as I put my hands back on her hips. "I'm pretty Goddamn irresistible." Tease gives me a weird look, which I ignore, before I turn her around and push her over. She groans, grabbing the edge of the cement with tense fingers, her ass out and ready for me. I take a split second to scope out her body, to memorize the wash of her red hair as it hangs down her back.

"No," Tease groans, but she doesn't move. "Stop." Her voice trails off and she drops her head, spreading her legs apart but staying right where she is. No doesn't always mean yes, but sometimes – it does.

I slide my cock into her swollen opening, and *fuck*. I almost come again right there in the hot, hot heat of her body. Even the water of the spa doesn't have a damn thing on this woman. Tease groans and presses back into me, using the cement wall of the tub to keep herself braced. As I start to thrust, water splashes every which way, emphasizing the smack of our bodies as I ram her as hard as I can. I get real deep, bury my dick inside her pussy as her body welcomes me, wrapping around my shaft like a glove.

I wrap my arm around her soft flesh and find her clit, swollen and waitin' desperately for me. As soon as I touch it, it's like a trigger goes off somewhere inside of her and she starts to scream.

"Oh, Beck," Tease groans as I increase the speed of my fingers and my hips, my balls slapping against her swollen pussy. Her moans echo around the cement area, probably drawin' attention from the nearby rooms. Oh, Lord help me. I could fall in love with a woman like this, so let the fuckers look. Let 'em look and weep because this little lady is mine tonight. "Oh, Beck. Oh, Beck. Oh, Beck, Oh, Beck. *Oh God.*" Tease sags in my arms as I slide my hand up to her belly and splay my fingers out on her smooth skin. She keeps moanin', her words drowned out by whimpers. Tease is letting herself go, completely and utterly, and I am fuckin' thrilled.

"So tight, Emilie. You are so, so fucking tight." Her

body feels like velvet against my cock, the skin of her ass soft and silky. The attraction between us is so hot, it scalds my damn skin where we're touching. I want to clutch her closer to me and push her away at the same damn time.

"I can't ... I ... " Tease groans, her voice falling and then rising in pitch as she tosses her red hair back and comes, body squeezin' tight against me, ridges grinding my cock into dust. My ass muscles clench and I release myself with a growl, coming inside of her as she spasms beneath me, fingers gripping the cement, ass up and out.

I stay where I am, panting hard, holding her up in the water as her hands slide down the wall and she ends up propped up by my arm. I can feel her pulse jumping as she struggles to find the energy to stand, pulling away from me with a groan, separating our bodies with an almost painful pop of energy. It don't feel right, her moving away from me. I grit my teeth and run my fingers through my hair.

"You are something else there, darlin'," I say as Tease scoots to the edge of the spa and climbs out onto the pavement, sitting down hard with a smack of her wet ass on the concrete. I grin as she sweeps hair from her face and looks at me hard, like she's delving in deep. Those green eyes spin through emotions faster than I can keep up with. No doubt about it; this girl is a hell of a lot smarter than I am.

"Thank you," she says, her voice confident and brazen despite her nakedness and her shaking hands. "And I guess ... so the fuck are you."

I laugh at her, but she doesn't look away, keeping her eyes locked on mine. Tease has got a gaze that feels a hell of a lot older than eighteen. Old soul in a young body. I think I might just be the opposite o' that. I've seen a lot in this life, but I feel like I came into it fresh. I almost wish me and Tease had met under different circumstances. I think we could've had a lot of fun together. She'd probably enjoy ridin' the country with Triple M.

The thought of my club sobers the moment up a bit, giving me just enough energy to take a step back and pull away from this girl and her magnetic half-smile.

We lived in the moment. Now it's time to see what the next one holds.

Tease
CHAPTER 14

Beck lets me shower, keeping his back turned while I scrub away the smell of chlorine and the feel of his hands on my body. But shame doesn't wash off that easily. I punch the wall of the shower, real quick, just to get out some frustration.

"You alright in there?" he asks me, but I don't turn around to see if he's looking at my body through the clear vinyl of the shower curtain. Apparently, I'm not able to control myself when he's around. My whole body is tight, pulled taut as a bowstring. If Beck were to pluck me, I'd let him play me all night long. Even though I shouldn't. *Traitor.* I slept with a murderer, a man who might be personally responsible for some of the deaths of my fellow club members and who is *definitely* guilty by association. And this time, I didn't do it to try and trick him, I did it just because. *Live in the moment.* I wish life were that easy.

Beck Evans makes everything seem so simple, so easy.

I finish showering and we switch places. He makes me sit on the toilet with a towel, but I don't bother to go anywhere. I'd have to have an incredible fucking plan to outrun or outmaneuver this man. It's fairly obvious at this point that he isn't going to hurt me, so why bother? I'll get back to Seventy-seven Brothers sooner or later. *There'll be funerals and angry faces, raised voices. My brother will send me back to the house with an armed guard, and then he'll hunt Triple M down and make them suffer.*

I pull the towel tight around my shoulders and force myself to keep my eyes on the wall in front of me. *Beck's muscles are so hard, so stiff underneath his tanned skin. And his cock is huge, so much bigger than the boys I dated in high school.* I touch my fingers to my lips and wish for a cigarette.

After he's done showering, Beck gives me some boxers and a shirt to sleep in. I feel so awkward being around him, but he just whistles as he digs some clothes out of his saddlebags. Again, I'm used to dating boys, not sleeping with *men*. And we're obviously not in a relationship. *Careful, Tease, your age is starting to show.*

"Are you really going to handcuff me?" I ask him as his hand emerges from the bag with a pair of metal cuffs. I imagine he's used these on a lot of women in the past. I highly doubt they're just for club business.

Beck swipes some wet hair from his forehead. He's walking around shirtless, drawing my eyes back to his body again and again and again. From the skull tattoo on his pecs to the delicious curve of his obliques as they disappear under the denim of his jeans, I am mesmerized.

"I got to, if either of us is going to be sleepin' tonight. Sorry to tell you this, Tease, but I am dead tired." He holds up the cuffs. "I'll make it as comfortable for you as I can. You've got my word on that."

I stand up from the chair I've been sitting in and move across the room, lying down on the bed with a sigh. Handcuffs. A double bed. Beck and me sleeping together on it. My heart starts to race. He helps me fluff the pillows, putting my head and neck into a comfortable position. The bed creaks as he kneels on it, a towering block of muscle and the sharp scent of spicy body wash I detected on him before. *Male.* That's what I smell from here, and it's like a drug. I can hardly think past it.

"Arms up," Beck says and I sigh as I lift my wrists over my head, feeling the cold metal slide around my skin. He doesn't just hook one wrist, but both of them, locking my hands together and then using a second pair – a *second* pair of cuffs – to attach me to the wooden post on the right side of the headboard. Right away, I feel that sense of vulnerability, that fear that he could do anything with me, *anything*, and I wouldn't be able to stop him. I don't like how excited I get down below.

Beck doesn't waste any time, flicking the lights off and curling up beside me, the roar of the highway a gentle sound in the distance. Headlights flash through our curtains every now and then, but for the most part, it's dark. I don't mind the dark, but tonight, it feels almost stifling. I can't keep my mind off of the day, replaying every single thing I did. *Such a failure.* Darren's probably so disappointed in me.

"Beck," I whisper, trying to determine if he's asleep or not. I adjust myself a bit and the metal on the handcuffs clinks. "Beck?" He rolls over with a groan, putting an arm across the bare bit of my belly that's showing beneath the shirt. I glance over at him and take a sharp intake of breath. His face is gorgeous in the near dark, a strong outline that emphasizes his nose, his perfect lips.

"What can I do ya for?" he asks me, voice already succumbing to sleep. I guess he must be exhausted. I know I am, but I can't keep my heart still. Adrenaline is pumping through my body, making my skin feel electric. I lick my lips, not sure what I was planning on saying.

"How is this really going to work? Once you trade me for your friend, what happens then? My brother won't let you go." Beck stays quiet, probably unaware of how heavy his arm feels on my belly, how warm, how much I wish I hated it being there. How I don't.

"I don't rightly know," he answers honestly. And then he laughs, his hot breath moving against the skin on my arm. "Probably won't end well, Tease. I won't lie to you. Honestly, I'd let ya go right now if I knew Melissa would be okay."

"Seventy-seven Brothers won't hurt her. That's not how we work. Other MCs maybe, but not us."

"Doesn't matter. We lost people; you lost people. Somebody has to pay. Until someone fesses up to the roof shooting, we're gonna be at a standstill."

"It wasn't us," I assure him, watching Beck sit up a bit, his muscular body a dark silhouette against the headboard. The loss of his arm on my stomach is frustrating, making me angry again. I refuse to acknowledge that the anger is directed more at myself than it is at him. I know what's going on here, and I know how ridiculous it is. *I'm crushing on Beck.* I started crushing on him the second I saw him, even when he was pulling my hair and growling against my face. I must have some serious issues. Beck is too old for me, first off. Second, we're worlds apart. Because of this situation, he could never be in Seventy-seven Brothers, and I could never be with someone who wasn't. We shouldn't even be ... living in the fucking moment.

"You keep saying that, but so what? It wasn't your guys, and it sure as fuck wasn't mine. Then who? We been over this, all of us. It's all my Pres is thinking about right now." Beck sighs and rubs at his face. As my eyes adjust to the dimness, I can see his face twisted in thought. "If there were someone who had a grudge against us, it would be a good play, but I can't think of anyone who's still breathing that would've had the opportunity. Unless we have a rat ... " His voice trails off, and I feel good, like I've planted a seed. Despite everything, I still want to help Triple M out. *Traitor.* Beck shakes his head and slumps back down, resting his arm behind his head.

The heat of his body warms mine, making me sweat, drawing drips of liquid down my skin, teasing my nerves with sensation. I want him to figure out who that shooter was because it *can't* have been my family. Darren isn't that stupid, and I can tell just from Beck's demeanor that they aren't either. Someone wanted us to fight. I don't have the information to figure out who, but maybe Beck can. If not him, then Darren. I *have* to talk to Darren.

"Tomorrow's another day," Beck whistles. "Hopefully a better one than today."

He lays back down, facing me. When I glance over at him, it looks like his eyes are closed. I shift uncomfortably, listening to the rattle of the handcuffs, feeling the sweat running down my body. Between my legs, an ache is pulsing, making me squeeze my thighs in desperation. Somehow not being able to move around, to touch my own body, makes me desperate to.

I stare at the ceiling and try to use my imagination to soothe my mind and body, imagining what would've happened if Beck had come into the club as a prospect, claimed me as his old lady … It's not as exciting as people-watching – it's much, much more entertaining.

"Is the air conditioning in here working?" I whisper, not knowing if he's asleep or if I should even bother him. Beck's laugh rumbles next to me.

"Are you hot, baby?" he asks me, and then he's leaning over, stubble brushing against my forehead as he presses his lips to my skin. My body bucks involuntarily, muscles seizing as a thrill rips straight through me. "Oh yeah, you're sweatin' like a sinner in church."

"Am I?" I ask him, completely and utterly aware of how close his body is to my own. I want him to press me into the bed with his weight, push my knees apart and slide into me. "Probably because I realize how stupid this is going to sound." I lick my lips. "Fuck me again?" I've already gone this far, so why not? Sleeping with him twice isn't any less terrible than doing it three times. *I'm such a fucking slut, a terrible fucking slut.* I like this though, this sex with no commitment. I don't have to worry that he's going to slap a jacket on my back and call me his own.

"Shoot," he snarls, fist curling in the pillow next to my head. "You didn't even need to ask." Beck sits up, suddenly wide awake, and settles himself between my legs. I fully expect him to undo the handcuffs.

He doesn't.

Instead he pulls the borrowed boxers off and tosses them to the floor. Before I can even utter a word, Beck is grabbing my hips and slamming his cock into me. He's so big, so so big. His dick opens my body up, spreading me wide. I lose my mind when I start fucking him, instincts taking over and forcing my thighs to spread as far open as I can.

"I was hopin' you'd give me an invitation, sweets," he says, pounding hard and fast. Our pelvises are slapping together, wet and warm. I guess I expected some slow foreplay, kissing or touching or ... whatever. But this is okay, too. Very okay.

"*Uh*," I groan, arching my back, straining my arms against the cuffs. My breasts are bouncing all over the place, my mind stretching to its limits. Beck is bruising my hips with his fingers, filling me and then leaving this empty gap that hurts so bad that it doesn't even matter that it's only a split second between thrusts. I keep moaning, thrashing back and forth, struggling even though I know I can't get free.

"Tease, you are so fuckin' hot," Beck tells me as I struggle to catch my breath, to find words. *So fast, happening so fast.* I'm absolutely drenched in sweat now, struggling to stay sane as pleasure arcs through my body. He's grinding into me so hard that all I can do is raise my chin and watch his muscles bunching and releasing. Claiming me. That's what it feels like. I try not to give in, even though I want to. *Oh, fuck me. Traitor, traitor, traitor.*

But then Beck just stops, pausing and freezing like a deer caught in the headlights. His body gets ramrod straight, his cock still trapped inside of me, keeping me open and wanting. A split second later, he leans over and strips a pillowcase from one of the pillows.

"What – " I start as Beck wraps the fabric around my head, gagging me. I'm so confused right now, my body an aching mess, my brain scrambling to understand what's going on here. Beck slides out of me with a whispered curse and moves over to the window, peering out the curtains with his bare ass hanging out of his jeans. I look around the room, absolutely baffled at his sudden change in behavior.

And worried. Really, really worried.

"Mother of Christ on high. Fuck." Beck turns and scoops up his saddlebags, drawing out a shirt and slipping it on before he starts to stuff fabric into the leather bag. I make some noises against the gag, rattle the handcuffs a little, but he doesn't look back at me. Instead, I watch as he moves like a shadow, gathering the few belongings that are scattered around. Ten seconds later, I hear voices outside in the parking lot. "Sorry about this, Tease," he says, and he does sound sorry, really sorry actually. Beck tucks his half-erect cock back in his pants and zips them up, fetching the discarded boxers and sliding them right up over my hips. My core is wet and hot, desperate and aching to be touched. But at the same time, I'm starting to wonder who's outside these curtains …

It could be my club, looking for me. The thought makes me happy even as it terrifies me. I don't want Beck dead, and if they find me here, especially like this, they will kill him. At the same time, I've seen this man move. What if he takes down someone I love with him? Right away, I know I'm not going to fight. I think of Lizzie back at the university and wonder what she would do in this situation. *Hell, she'd probably run away and marry this man. That would be a Lizzie move for sure.*

I watch as Beck uncuffs me from the bed, but leaves my wrists shackled; he doesn't bother to remove the gag either. With his bags draped over one arm, Beck reaches underneath me and lifts me off the bed, moving over to the window and peering out the curtains again. I can't see much from where I'm at, but I can hear the voices a little better. Men. A lot of them. I can't tell how many because they're talking in low tones – at least three, possibly a lot more. Could be my brothers in arms or not. From the way Beck's acting though, I'd say it was a definite possibility.

He waits for awhile and then creeps over to the door, hoisting me into one arm and then using the other to remove the chain and twist the deadbolt. His face is dead serious, no hint of a smile on that face. Beck's almost scary like this. If I hadn't been around men twice as stern, I might be worried.

"This is going to be quick, and probably not a lot of fun. Whatever you choose to do right now, I won't hold it against you, darling." He looks down at me and we make eye contact. I don't know what he can see in my gaze, but whatever it is, it spurs him out the door in an instant, moving across the pavement at a run. His motorcycle's parked just a few doors down, under an awning and stuffed between a white van and a blue pickup truck.

I'm pretty sure that's the only thing that saves him.

"Who the fuck is that?" I hear someone snap as we barrel down the sidewalk in a blur. Beck only pauses for an instant to throw my arms around his neck, so that I'm facing him, still handcuffed, still gagged. We straddle the motorcycle as a pair of men in leather jackets come around the back of the van. Flying my club's colors. It's Cape and Tim. I can tell right away.

"It's Tease!" Tim screams, pulling out his gun and aiming for Beck's back tire. Too late he fires off a shot as the engine revs up and we go screaming over the curb and onto the sidewalk. My hair flaps in Beck's face as the motorcycle grinds through the walkway and explodes onto the street, men in leather shouting behind us. I can see them over Beck's shoulder as we move away, racing down the parking lot, carrying guns and hammers and wrenches. But they can't fire at Beck because they might hit me. *I'm sorry, Darren*, I call out in my head, hoping that somehow, he knows I didn't want this to happen. Even though I'm enjoying Beck, even though I *shouldn't* be enjoying Beck. I just want to see his face and make sure he's alright.

"Goddamn it," Beck snarls because he knows the chase isn't over. Not by a long shot. A few seconds later, the growling roar of hogs starts up not too far behind us. I don't think it's a full group, not the usual seventy-seven my brother sends out on official club business, but at least a dozen based on the noise.

My hair continues to fly around in wild bursts of red, smacking Beck's face and hopefully not impairing his vision overly much. If we go down, dressed like this, we're going to be shredded alive on the pavement.

Beck picks up speed, using his little Suzuki to his advantage, tearing around corners, and flying off the beaten path, into a grassy patch and around some trees. It's a risky move because if they see where he's going, they'll catch up to us for sure. That, or we could easily hit a pothole, a fallen log, anything, and go down hard. I close my eyes for a moment, letting time freeze briefly around me.

The wind feels good against my skin and the rush of adrenaline isn't unwelcome. My heart is pounding faster now than it ever has before, pounding against my ribcage so loud, I'm sure Beck can feel it, too. It's a surreal split in time where nothing means everything – the little white farmhouse across the highway, the split in the trees, the silver light of the moon beaming down on us. It all feels symbolic. I close my eyes and let go, trying to accept that whatever happens is going to happen. At this second, I am not in control. I'm honestly not ever really in control.

"Fucking Christ on a cracker," Beck growls, spinning the bike in a dangerous arc and and sliding to a stop next to a dilapidated barn. He kills the engine right away and waits, his chest rising and falling in a rapid rhythm, straining against mine from where I'm pressed against him, legs wrapped around his waist. I've been in the club my whole life, ridden a lot of choppers, but I don't think I've ever sat like this. "Come on, come on, come on," he whispers, eyes flicking back and forth, examining the highway. I watch, too, listening for the roar of engines. My heart stops briefly as they move past us, flying down the dark highway at staggering speeds. Country dark isn't like city dark though. There are no streetlights, hardly any porch lights. We're buried in plain sight right here, and for all they know, Beck is still on the road straight ahead. He made a smart choice driving through the break in the hedges on this property, straight through the grass. Other than a small track mark, nearly invisible in the silver light of the moon, there's no sign we even came this way.

Beck sits back with a sigh of relief, putting his hands on the curve of my waist.

"That was a fucking close one," he says, sweat pooling on his upper lip. He flicks it away with his tongue. "How the fuck did they find us anyway?" he wonders aloud. I make a noise under the gag, but Beck just chuckles. "Can't remove that yet, Miss Emilie. I'm sorry about that, but you've got a vested interest in the enemy." I make a grunting noise that clearly tells him to fuck off. How stupid does he think I am? I don't want them to find me yet. I need to talk to Darren, see if he can find out anything about the shooter. That, and Beck needs more time to think. If we can work this out so that neither club is to blame, then when it comes time for the switch, maybe we can arrange it so that nobody gets hurt. It's a long shot, but I have to try. I have to. "Obviously, I let my guard down a bit. Can't let that shit happen again." Beck scratches at the back of his head. When his eyes come back to mine, trailing down my face and focusing on my lips, I find it hard to swallow. Or maybe it's just the gag in my mouth. "You, missy, are a distraction." I pull hard on his neck, but he doesn't budge. Beck Evans is like a rock.

His hands move down my body, cupping my ass, sliding forward and touching the bare skin on my thighs. Almost unconsciously, I drop my legs from around his waist and open wider. Beck licks his lips, eyes darting back towards the highway. The sound of the motorcycles is a distant roar now. I don't think they know we're here, and by the time they figure out we're not in front of them and circle back, it'll be too late. There are a million side roads to nowhere out here.

"You damn near got me killed," Beck says, dropping his fingers to the fabric of the boxers and then sliding them down until he touches the bare skin of my inner thighs. I moan and arc my hips, naturally moving towards him and the growing bulge in his pants. The lust I feel for this man is like an unstoppable force. It's scaring the crap out of me, to be honest. But what am I going to do? I've never felt anything like this in my whole life, and I don't know how to fight it. "Damn near got me killed," he repeats, unzipping his pants and freeing his cock. It springs forward like it's got a mind of its own, straining for me, desperate to be inside. I close my eyes so tight they hurt and then open them again, finding Beck's dark gaze in the moonlight. His face is covered in shadow, carving out spots where his cheekbones are, his eyes, his lips. It's a little eerie, but in a sexy, mysterious sort of way.

Beck pulls me forward with one hand on my ass, leaving the handcuffs hooked around his neck, the gag still in my mouth, and then he guides his cock to the fly on the boxers, moving aside the fabric and brushing the head of it against my swollen heat. My eyes flutter and my heart quickens as I open wider and welcome him in again, taking the entire length of his shaft in one stroke. I'm still soaking wet from our half-session on the bed.

"Goddamn it," Beck whispers roughly, letting me rock my hips into him, setting the rhythm at slow and sensual. The gag doesn't stop me from moaning, but no actual words come out, just desperate sounds and soft cries. The angle we're at is almost painful, letting him delve all the way inside of me, filling me up and splitting me open. He's so thick it almost hurts, makes me wish I could open my legs even wider. One of his hands stays firmly cupped on my ass; the other makes its way up my shirt, feeling my breast with calloused fingers, massaging my nipple with nearly painful pressure.

I cry out and the gag fills my mouth, the fabric heavy with saliva. I want it *gone*, and I want it gone now, but I have no way of telling Beck that, so I get angry again. My hips rock harder as he stares down at me, mouth slightly parted, groans slipping from his throat unashamedly. I move as fast as I can, my stomach muscles cramping in protest as I gyrate my hips forward, letting my head fall back while the cuffs keep me upright. Warm night air kisses my skin as Beck lifts my shirt, dropping his head to my tits, tasting my nipple with his hot breath. His teeth graze the sensitive pink skin, rolling it around in his mouth as his hand tightens on my ass, fingers digging into the fabric of the boxer shorts.

"Make me come, Tease. Do it. Show me what you got." I keep moving my hips, letting my entire upper body relax back, hair hanging in a red curtain past my shoulders. I match the rhythm of my movement to Beck's grunts, feeling a surge of excitement when he starts to move against me. "Milk me like a motherfuckin' cow, baby," he drawls. "Draw it all out of me." I kick up my pace as his mouth moves between my breasts and then up, pushing the shirt out of the way so he can lick my collarbone and kiss the hollow of my throat.

When he stops, I almost go crazy. My head snaps up and I glare at him as he pulls out of me with a slight smirk and a chuckle. His hand moves down to his shaft and starts stroking, moving slow at first and then quicker until he's groaning and coming all over my chest. My breasts are heaving and my body is in absolute complete and utter turmoil. I speak against the gag, but nothing audible comes out.

"You're done, too?" Beck asks with another laugh and a shake of his head. "Good thing, too, because we need to get the hell out of here." I squeeze my legs together, trapping him between my thighs, but he still doesn't make any move to keep touching me. Instead, he reaches up and removes my arms from around his neck, pushing me off of him and standing up in the knee-high grass around us. I mouth some curses against my gag, but Beck ignores me, zipping up his pants and then glancing back over at the road.

I pull my shirt down awkwardly, the cuffs jangling loudly in the country air.

"Just a minute there, sweet thing. I'm trying to think up

the best plan here. Don't want to start up my bike and draw any unwanted attention." Beck licks his lips and then moves over to the darkened house behind us, leaving me alone on his motorcycle. I swing my leg over and stumble off, moving after him with angry steps. He peers into the windows of the house and takes a step back, just as I slam him in the back with both fists, reaching up and grabbing the gag from my mouth.

"Fuck you," I snarl, right before he spins around, grabs me around the waist and pulls me close to him. Our bodies are pressed tightly together, his arms strong and solid around me. It's an interesting sensation, different than the sex but still exciting, still enough to make my heart pound. "That was just downright *rude*," I tell him, feeling his seed on my chest, wishing I could wipe it off and slap him. Wishing that I didn't like it. *This is not the Tease I know*, I tell myself. *What is wrong with you? Get ahold of yourself and remember why you're here: he kidnapped you. And now you have a responsibility to your club to limit the damage done on this end.*

Beck grins at me, nice and wide.

"I wasn't done, sugar love. I just wanted to make sure the house was empty before I did this." Beck scoops me up in his arms again, moving us back over to the bike and sitting me in the grass next to it. "Thought it might be weird if somebody were to walk out on us." Beck kisses my mouth hard and then pushes me back into the grass. "But the house is vacant. Your lucky day."

"Are you going to take off the handcuffs?" I ask him as he kneels down, making me wonder where this is going. I have an idea, but I've never gone that route before, so I don't know what to expect. Beck leans over me, still smiling. A few minutes ago, he was running for his life. You'd never know it now by just looking at him. I guess he really does believe in his *live in the moment* motto.

"I can't, baby doll. I'm sorry. What happens if they come back and I have to make another run for it? I like you, but I also don't know that I could trust you to cooperate." Beck grabs at the waistband on the boxers as I lay there with green surrounding me on all sides, a wall of foliage blocking out the highway and the occasional car.

"But you're still willing to take a break here and have sex with me?" I wonder as he strips the boxers down and puts them aside. The questions disintegrates in an instant as Beck grabs my legs and pushes my knees back, dropping his head and pressing a quick kiss to my inner thigh.

"Like I said, you damn near got me killed. I barely have a lick of sense when it comes to you."

"So, handcuffs then?" I ask, jingling the metal around, pretending my face isn't flushed and my hands aren't shaking. I've never had anyone go down on me before. It's just not something that teenage boys are generally interested in. At least neither of the ones I dated were. I can almost forgive Beck for … coming on me.

He laughs at me again and settles himself in, relaxing down there like this isn't an intimate experience for me. My eyes stare up at the branches of a tree and a dark wash of sky, peppered with silver stars. As soon as he starts to kiss down my leg, I stop him, squeezing my thighs together against his head.

"You alright?" he asks, drawing back and looking at me, at my pursed lips, my red cheeks. "Something wrong?" Beck's voice changes, gets deeper. There's an intense focus in him as he raises up to his elbows and lets his eyes roam the space around us.

"I'm sorry. I don't think I can do this."

"You can't do what, Tease?" he asks, sounding genuinely baffled. I struggle to sit up without the use of my hands. Beck ends up wrapping his fingers around the chain of the cuffs and pulling me forward. Immediately I put my hands between my legs, cutting off his view.

"This. Oral sex. I don't … know you. I'm sorry, but I can't do this." One of his red brows raises up, but he doesn't say anything. I sigh and slump forward, my body still tight and desperate for release but also tired. I'm bordering on exhaustion at this point. "Can we go now?"

"Well, we're staying here tonight, Tease. This is going to be our bed." Beck slaps at the grass with the palm of his hand. "But if you don't want any lovin', I ain't gonna force you." I swallow hard and try to figure out why I'm being such a baby about this. I let him put his dick inside of me, but I'm having trouble imagining him putting his face down there. It doesn't make any sense. Lizzie would say I'm sexually confused, that all the time I've spent with Seventy-seven Brothers has warped my views on relationships and physical expression. She was a firm, firm believer that the club was no good for women. I see all her points, and sitting here right now, I guess she was right in a way. But the MC is home, family. We'd all die for each other. We all have each other's backs. Not many people have that kind of support. But then I think of the Mamas, the women that work in the clubhouse cleaning and cooking alongside the prospects, bringing in money on the side, keeping the boys entertained. And getting almost nothing in return for it. What kind of life is that?

I want to belong, but maybe that's not the right place for me. I'm not judging others, but for me ... I blink away the thoughts and focus on Beck. He's examining me now, giving me a strange look.

"Think you can get it up again?" I ask, trying to turn his attention away from my refusal and onto something else. Beck grins big and wide, moving up against me until our hips are matched, hands pressed into the ground on either side of my face.

"You kiddin' me? I was just trying to do you a favor. If this is what you want instead, I'm game." I hook my arms back around his neck, spreading my legs open and welcoming the hard press of Beck's cock inside his denim jeans. He nuzzles my neck, almost affectionately, and presses a few searing kisses against my throat. "Maybe I can use the next couple o' days to work you up to it. What do you say? I can't let you leave without tasting all of my special Beck bullshit."

"I'm not sure how to respond to that," I tell him as he reaches down and unzips his jeans, moving to find my opening again. We just keep fucking and fucking. I don't know what it is between us. I don't think I even did it this much with my high school boyfriends.

"Just say you'll think about it. As my captive, you owe me that much at least, don't you?" His chuckle turns into a groan as I arch my hips up, sliding against his body. "Alright, alright, Miss Hathorne. Hold your horses. I got your back, baby." Beck settles himself on top of me, kissing my mouth, tangling his fingers in my hair. I return the favor, managing to stroke my fingers through the silky red even with my wrists bound tight. My tongue meets his, sliding slick inside his hot mouth. His kisses feel so real, like there's something more behind them than just sex. I know it isn't true, but the fact that he can make me feel this way confirms what I already knew. *Men kiss differently than boys. Boys slather your mouth with saliva; men capture your soul.*

Smooth as a damn criminal, Beck thrusts inside of me again, merging his warm body with mine. The sensation of his naked cock inside of me turns my insides to jelly and my brain to mush. The difference between a condom and bare flesh is subtle, but powerful. I feel like there's an unbroken current circulating between our bodies, speeding my heart, quickening my breath. When he starts pounding me into the dirt and the overgrown grass, I'm already halfway there.

My body goes numb and my eyes roll back, lashes fluttering as I let myself sink into the ground, melding with Beck's hard muscles. My legs go around him, ankles locking against his ass.

"Come for me, baby. 'S your turn now." Beck bites down on my lower lip, grinding into me, pushing me off the precipice and over the edge. When I fall, the pleasure coiling at the base of my spine explodes and my voice rings out through the emptiness all around us.

Tease
CHAPTER 15

When I wake up, face pressed into the dirt, body so sore I can hardly move, the cuffs are gone and there's a T-shirt draped over my bare butt. I groan as I struggle to sit up, clutching the fabric tight. Not that it should matter. Beck's seen it all now. Still, it doesn't seem right. A flurried frenzy of locking bodies is different than just being comfortably naked around someone, isn't it?

"What time is it?" I ask, blinking at the dappled sunshine streaming through the leaves of the tree above me. I rub at my eyes and then run both hands down my face. I've lived in the same house for eighteen years. Other than the clubhouse, and a sparse few vacations in my younger years, I haven't slept anywhere but in my own bed. Waking up on the ground outside of an abandoned farmhouse is beyond strange.

Beck takes another drag on his cigarette and turns to face

me, perched on the seat of his motorcycle. There's a massive grin plastered across his lips as he holds out his hand and passes the cigarette to me. I try not to grasp desperately at it, but fuck. I haven't had one since early yesterday. My hands shake as I lift the smoke to my sore lips. They feel stamped, marked, like Beck left some sort of symbol plastered across them. I poke at the tender flesh with my fingers as I inhale.

"'Bout that time," he says, and then swings his leg over so that he's straddling the bike. I'm used to the custom choppers my brothers build back home, but I can appreciate the speed and easy handling of Beck's ride. It might not be the fanciest bike I've ever seen, but it's perfectly maintained. If I didn't know better, I'd say it was brand new. Something looks a little different about it though, like maybe someone's done some tinkering around. They'd have to, I guess, because Beck is a big man and he probably weighs a whole hell of a lot with all that muscle. *You should know, Tease. You've felt his weight crushing you into the dirt, his body diving deep into yours.* I brush the thoughts away, letting them drift into the warm air like smoke. "Somethin' my momma used to say. Took me till I was twenty-six to figure that shit out." Beck watches me for a moment and then checks his phone. "It's twelve thirty, for those of y'all that require the little details in life." He chuckles and sits up straight, slapping his palms on his thighs as I glance around and spot the boxer shorts lying next to me.

"So, we were cruising pretty fast last night," I start,

grabbing the fabric and tugging the boxers over my ankles. Beck's eyes fall on my body, eating me up with a hungry gaze that I ignore. If we fuck again right now, I might not be able to walk. That, and there's a lot more traffic on the highway this morning than there was last night. "How's that even possible with a bike that small?" I stand up, stumbling a bit and flushing when Beck reaches out to grab my hand. "You must weigh a lot. Add me on there and I'm surprised we even broke fifty miles an hour. How the hell did you manage to outrun my club?"

Beck's grin gets even wider as he releases my fingers, almost reluctantly, and pats the side of his ride.

"Shoot, I feel like I'm ridin' a damn tricycle on this thing sometimes." He gets out another cigarette and leans back, looking down at his motorcycle with a gentle fondness. I've never understood that bond, even growing up surrounded by bikes. I enjoy them, am fascinated by them, but I've never fallen in love like that with a piece of metal. Hell, I've never even fallen in love with a person like that before. "And yeah, you're right. Factory condition, it would've barely gotten us down the damn interstate at grandma speed. But I got a friend, Mireya, that's balls to the wall genius on this shit. She tinkered around with it some."

I reach over and grab my jacket from on top of Beck's saddlebags. He left a pair of jeans there, too, and a belt. Not mine, but definitely not a woman's either. They're probably his. I could fit both legs into one, but I doubt in that rushed frenzy last night that he remembered to pack my wet jeans.

The pink flip flops managed to come along for the ride though. I start putting on the pants while Beck chuckles at me.

"I do look ri-damn-diculous on this fuckin' thing, don't I? It sort of started off as a joke and well, here we are today, still together after all these fucking years." Beck laughs again, loud and raucous, like he seems to do a lot, flipping his phone around in his hand and checking the screen. "Sometimes you don't get to choose your partner. Life chooses it for you." Chills grip my spine, making me stand stiff and straight as I struggle to find a hole on the belt that will actually keep these pants up. No such luck. They end up slipping down my hips as I clutch at the denim with tense fingers. I don't know what's wrong with me, why such an innocuous phrase has my stomach tight and my breath fluttering like the butterflies coalescing near the base of the tree.

"Any news?" I ask Beck, swallowing hard and trying to maintain that neutral expression I'm so good at. It's weird, but when he glances over me, gaze raking down the baggy shirt I'm wearing, to the laughably ill fitting pants, I feel naked, exposed. Much more so than when I'm at the clubhouse wearing a metal bra and leather shorts. I can't make sense of it, so I don't bother to try.

"Well, your brother is pissed the fuck off after last night. I guess your friends caught a gander at the cuffs and the gag." Beck shrugs and finishes off his cigarette. His red hair is brilliant in the sunshine, a shade lighter than mine. If I had to name the colors, I'd say he had ruby red and I had red wine. Subtle, but definitely different. "And before you even ask, I'll tell you. The man my Pres spoke with was named Tax. Do we have the right guy?" My heart swells and I nearly collapse with relief. I assumed that Darren was okay, but knowing for sure, that makes me feel a hell of a lot better. "Guess so," Beck drawls when I don't answer. "After what he saw," he continues, voice losing some of its humor. "He's not so happy with us. And Austin's not so happy with him. We had an arrangement to meet in a week, but your guys are still trolling around looking for you."

"So what happens now?" I ask as Beck tosses the pink flip flops at my feet. He grins again. It seems like it's almost impossible to keep the expression off of his face. It's okay though, at least for me, because I don't mind it. Makes the world seem a little less bleak.

"Now you get to meet the club."

My heart stops.

"Triple M?" I ask, even though I know that's exactly what he means. This strange, nomadic club with their weird rules and their women in patches. On their own bikes. With balls of steel. I almost feel physically sick. I've been weirdly obsessed with them for awhile now, weaving fantasies in my brain. Meeting Beck was strange enough, but to see the entire group, colors flying, eyes narrowed on me. I blink a couple of times to clear my head. There's a good chance they could blame me for the deaths of their club members. Beck has already told me he wouldn't touch me without my permission, but what about the rest of the club?

"You alright there, Miss Emilie?" I look at him and steel my expression. Whatever happens, I can deal. Just like I was willing to sleep with Beck to try and escape, I can take anything they throw at me, just as long as it keeps more people from losing their lives. I can sacrifice myself for the good of Seventy-seven Brothers and die happy for it. *Can't I?*

"I'm fine," I tell him as he reaches out and grabs me by the wrists, hauling me forward and pulling me into his arms. Like we're friends instead of strangers. It's a little unnerving. Beck breathes in my hair and laughs against my scalp, pulling out some stray strands of grass with his fingers.

"You don't look fine. You look like you swallowed a damn cactus, and down the wrong pipe, too. Listen here, Miss Emilie, I told you, you ain't got nothing to worry about with me. Nobody in Triple M's gonna rough you up, babe."

I smile, but I'm not a hundred percent certain that I believe him. I guess I'll be finding out soon enough. I take a step back and struggle to keep the loose jeans from falling down my hips. I have a feeling that if they do, Beck and I might just forget about other things and climb back in the grass.

"Thank you, Beck. You've been a pretty gracious fucking kidnapper." He laughs again and scoots forward on his ride, patting the seat behind him.

"Well, thank you, sugar. You've been a mighty fine kidnap victim, if I do say so myself. Now, hop on. I can trust you not to leap off mid-ride?"

"I've given up trying to escape at this point, Beck." My smile gets a little more real, and he nods his head. I can tell he hears the truth in my voice. I could escape, maybe, if I kept trying. It seems like despite his words last night, he is starting to trust me. The question I have for myself is: do I want to betray that trust?

CHAPTER 16

"Whatcha listening to back here, boss?" I drawl, moving through the Triple M'ers guarding the back gate and pausing in an overgrown yard. I have to admit, I rode by the place twice before Kimmi flagged me down, dressed in a black leather corset and short shorts. Tease's eyes immediately locked onto my best good friend and haven't moved since. Granted, we just climbed off the fuckin' bike and walked in here, but still. I think she's impressed. I grin. Kimmi certainly makes an interesting impression on folks.

"*Scar Tissue*," Austin drawls right back, dropping his head, so that he can stare at me from his position on a lounge chair. Doesn't look like he's been doin' much lounging though. His face is drawn and tight and his muscles are stiff as a dead man's. He's slumped there, but he's anything but relaxed. "By the Red Hot Chili Peppers."

"Oh come the fuck on, brother," I laugh as I move

154

forward, stepping over a cracked angel statue with a missing head. My heart is racing like crazy, but I'm tryin' to keep my cool. Being separated from the gang was odd. I ain't been away from these stupid fuckers for a long time, especially not in times o' crisis. Now I have to come in and look at these faces and count the ones that aren't here anymore. My hands squeeze into fists, and I can almost feel the ink drilled into my flesh. *Hopeless.*

"I thought you'd be happy it wasn't Nickelback again," Austin groans, rising to his feet. He's got a beer in his right hand, but it doesn't look like he's taken a single sip of it. We hug each other briefly and take a step back, his eyes going straight to Tease. I step to the side so Austin can get a good look at her, wearing her leather jacket and my baggy jeans. She looks ridiculously beautiful. I don't think she has a fuckin' clue how good. I stifle my raging hormones and get out a cigarette, trying to keep this as civil as possible. There's going to be some animosity towards Tease, no doubt about it. People fuckin' *died* yesterday. But I also promised that nothing was going to happen to her and I meant it.

"Austin Sparks, this is Emilie Hathorne." I pause as her green eyes shift over to mine. "But you can call her Tease." Austin just stands there, his expression virtually unreadable. He's stressing out, I can tell. Thank the fuckin' stars I'm back today. Time to whip his ass back into shape.

"You're still alive? Damn. I was hoping I'd never have to see your ass again," Mireya says, moving down the steps from the house and pausing on the patio. I toss her a wink that she smiles at, and wait for Gaine to come over and give me another bro hug. If you're scared to hug your brothers, you got some serious issues. Work that shit out.

His turn to look at Tease. Right away, a frown tweaks his face. He ain't happy with me. I know he knows we slept together. Perceptive little fucker. Kimmi's probably the only one that won't mind. Think she might've been checking Tease out.

"Goddamn it, Beck," Gaine whispers under his breath, exchanging a look with Austin. My friend rubs at the blonde stubble on his chin and shakes his head, turning his attention back to Tease and her hot mess of an outfit. I'll have to get one of the girls to lend her some clothes. I'm almost scared to though. Imagine if she looks that good in an ugly ass outfit how she's going to look in tight pants and a wife-beater. I reach down and adjust myself, getting yet another scowl from Gaine, the Goddamn fairytale fucking princess. I think he's slept with maybe three ladies since he joined the club. I don't know who's happier that he and Mireya got hitched – them or me.

"What?" I ask him, holding out my arm to indicate the gorgeous girl by my side. "We have a mutual attraction is all." I try to keep my voice down, but I'm sure the word will spread. That's okay though. Ain't a single soul here man enough to say anything to my face. Well, except for these stupid fuckers.

"I knew it," Kimmi hisses, diamond earrings swinging as she steps up on my right side and puts her hands around my bicep. "You did fuck her. I knew you were a slut, but sleeping with the enemy? Desperate much?" I just laugh and reach over, curling my arm around Tease's waist and dragging her against me. She looks almost as shocked as Austin.

"Boy meets girl and magic happens, lady love. Get over yourself. Y'all are just jealous."

"Jealous is hardly the word I was lookin' for," Austin says, meeting Tease's gaze. "I know you weren't there, but we suffered yesterday."

"So did we," she replies, chin raised, already in defense mode. "You lost ten; we lost eight. And I still don't know the names of my fallen brothers, so I can grieve properly. I'm not here to start trouble. My only goal is to get this worked out without more blood being shed."

Austin stands stone still, brown eyes so focused on Tease's that I start to get worried. I don't know what he's going to ask me to do with her. I won't sit around and watch her be ridiculed or beat up or nothin' like that. But I also don't want to defy my President, especially not when his hold on the group is so tenuous, when any-fucking-thing could happen.

"I also wanted to ask you if I could speak with my President." *Goddamn this girl never gives up, does she*? "I think there's a strong possibility that the person who shot your club member wasn't a part of either MC. I need to let him know my thoughts." Tease runs her tongue over her lower lip. "I swear on Seventy-seven Brothers that I won't say a thing about your position. My only interest at this point is in ending this peacefully."

"Well spoken, sugar tits," I laugh, but nobody's laughing alongside me. That's alright, happens all the damn time. Austin stands there in silence, examining this girl like he isn't sure what to think. In my opinion, Tease has got a little bit of that same quiet rebellious streak that Amy has. I think if he gives her a chance, the two of them could be friends. Kimmi leans forward and peers around me, mouth slightly parted, eyes curious. Tease glances over at her, and I notice that her eyes take in Kimmi's fingers on my arm. She don't like it, not one fuckin' bit. *What the hell is going on here?*

"Alright," Austin says, surprising the hell out of me. "Come with me, and I'll let you make the call."

"What the hell?" I ask, releasing my arm from around Tease's waist and following after them into the house. It's mostly empty in here, filled with sleeping bags and blankets. Looks like we're camping out, I guess. It's good cover, but I can't imagine that anyone's happy holed up in here. We need to take care of this shit sooner rather than later. At least the bikes are hidden in the three car garage out back. That's a nice fuckin' feature. Now that Kent's gone and fucked up our shit, I'm starting to wonder if it isn't time for a clubhouse. Triple M's always been nomadic, and that's worked for us, but now, it might be time to take a different approach.

I run my hand through my hair as Austin leads us to the kitchen, pausing next to Amy and Christy. They both turn to look at Tease. Christy's still got that scared shitless look on her face, but Amy smiles.

"Hi," she says, taking in Tease's odd outfit with sympathy. "Amy Cross." She holds out her hand while Austin looks on possessively, body tense like he thinks Tease is going to hurt his precious little lady. *What a goofy bastard.*

"Tease," Emilie says, introducing herself and shaking Amy's hand in a firm grip. Her gaze is open and calculating. I can only wonder what she's thinking about. Seems like you either love or hate our group. Somehow I find myself caring about Tease's opinion, like it even matters if she approves of us or not. "It's nice to meet you, Amy." Tease gives her a smile, too, and steps forward to accept the cellphone in Austin's outstretched fingers.

"Two minutes or less. Don't make me regret this," he tells her, moving up to Amy and putting his hands on either side of her hips. Tease licks her lips again and dials a number from memory, lifting the phone up to her face. I notice that she refuses to meet my eyes while she's waiting for an answer. It's a small thing, shouldn't mean anything to me. Tease is just another little bunny in my bed, but she sure as hell knows how to grab my attention. I find myself with my hands on my hips, waiting for the call to be finished, just so we can lock eyes again.

"Tax, it's Tease," she says and her voice gets soft. I can tell she loves her brother, but that she's also a bit scared of 'im. There's no emotional outburst from either side, at least not that I can hear, but Tease's breathing speeds up and her hand fists in her shirt. "I'm fine, really. It wasn't what it looked like." I grin again and notice a few sets of eyes turning to look my way. *Oh, hell yeah it was.* "Tax, I think there's more to this shooting than first meets the eye." Tease glances up and meets Austin's stern expression. "I don't think it was anyone from Triple M." Another pause. "I can't, Tax. I tried, but it doesn't seem like a possibility." Tease cringes, like maybe she ain't used to standing up to her brother. Wouldn't surprise me at all. Look at the back of her jacket. I let my eyes trace the pair of sevens there, the patches that proclaim who she belongs to. Bothers me a little. I don't have a fuckin' clue why, but I get the strongest urge to rip it off her shoulders then. *Fuck.*

I continue to smoke my cigarette, nodding my head at Triple M'ers and winking at some of the ladies. The general feeling in the air here is anger, rage. Frustration. Triple M wants vengeance; Seventy-seven Brothers wants vengeance. This is not going to turn out well, is it? *Shoot.*

"Tax, I think we can make a clean exchange." Tease looks at Austin and then holds out the phone, her lips pursed and her facial expression unreadable. He takes it from her with a nervous flick of his tongue over his lower lip.

"You should listen to your sister. Clean exchange, no blood shed." Austin pauses. "I don't know what else you want me to say to you, sir. I'm tryin' to be polite here, but it isn't easy." Austin takes a step away from Amy and leans against the peeling wallpaper at his back. "Let me talk to my crew and see what I can come up with." And then he hangs up.

Gaine and I exchange a glance. Tease remains motionless, almost completely frozen. The jeans are sagging down her hips, but she doesn't make any move to lift them up. Her blinking eyes are the only sign of life that I can see.

"Can I talk to y'all for a moment?" Austin asks, looking at Tease and then over at Mireya. Gaine's wife rolls her eyes and shakes her head, throwing her hands up in the air and cursing in Spanish.

"Why has my whole life been reduced to taking care of runaway bitches?"

"Mireya," Austin warns, but she ignores him.

"*Madre Mia.* What a joke. I get to dress up the enemy's ol' lady." Mireya lights up a cigarette and tucks some dark hair behind her ear, giving Tease a dirty once-over. "Might as well get you out of those clothes, honey." Mireya's dark eyes move over to mine, and I grin at her hard, wishin' like hell that the next thing out of her mouth wasn't going to be caustic as a hog's piss. "From the looks of you, it doesn't seem like that's a very difficult task."

"What the fuck did you just say to me, bitch?" Tease explodes, turning into a very different woman than the one I spent the day with yesterday. Some of that pride, that fierce loyalty to her MC, it all explodes in a rush.

"What, you thought sleeping with Beck would get you special treatment? You're our prisoner here, so whether you like it or not, you're going to take my shit. You can be *my* old fucking lady while you're here."

"Whoa there," I say, stepping between the two of them before a fight can break out. Mireya looks like she wants it *bad*. I don't know if she sees some of herself in Tease maybe. Could be old guilt and pain coming out right now, so I try not to be angry. As an emotion, it's generally useless. Won't get you nowhere that a hard right hook and a mean grin can't achieve. "No need for squabbles. Just get the girl some clothes and try to be nice. Remember where you come from, Mireya," I say, touching Tease's arm. She pulls it away from me, suddenly uncomfortable in the midsts of all these people. Granted, most of the club is hanging out in the doorways and watching. Our green gazes meet, but Tease doesn't give me anything in her look. "Chin up there, sugar," I tell her as Mireya rolls her eyes and turns on the heel of her boot, moving towards the hallway in the back. Tease pulls her attention away from me and follows after. I hope like hell there isn't going to be an explosion back there. We've had enough cat fights as of late. I like 'em as much as the next guy, but if I ain't around to watch ... You know, if a tree falls in the forest and nobody's around to hear it, does it make sound? It's that sorta thing, ain't it?

"What are we discussing?" Gaine asks as Austin moves back into the yard and retrieves his beer from the arm of the lounge chair. Kimmi and I follow along after him, and wait in a semi-circle while Austin takes a drink. "Who's going to take the fall for the shooting? Because I thought we were done with that."

"Take the fall?" I ask, scratching my chin. "What the hell are you talking about?"

"Seventy-seven Brothers wants somebody to step forward and take responsibility. We surrender that person to their mercy, give 'em back the girl, and they promise us a two day head start." Austin shakes his head as he says this, like he can't even believe we ended up in this position.

"What kind of shitty ass deal is that? We have to sacrifice yet another innocent club member just to appease them?" I scoff and reach out for the beer, snatching it from his hand and downing the rest of the liquid in a single gulp. If I had the time or leisure, I would be gettin' shit faced tonight. There're too many damn emotions swirling around in my fuckin' head. Worst part about it is, the main concern that's driftin' through my gray matter has nothing to do with clubs or deals or any of that shit. It's Tease. "Fuckin' Christ on a cracker," I swear, moving over to a table and snagging another beer. At least it looks like there's plenty to go around.

"That's not what he's asking for this time though," Austin says, ruffling his sandy hair with his fingers. "Right now he's asking for a straight up exchange, Tease for Melissa. I guess he and his boys saw something last night that's got him up in arms. We do a straight trade, and then they give us a day's head start. After that, the gauntlets are thrown and we're in a full on war." My friend glares at me, but I just shrug, the leather of my jacket crinkling.

"Honestly, how's that any worse than what he wanted before? In my opinion, it's a hell of a lot better. You should be thanking me."

"Beck, seriously?" Gaine asks, fuckin' hoity-toity little dreamer that he is. "How could you sleep with that girl? Her people *killed* ten of yours. Ten."

"Believe it or not, Gaine, casual sex doesn't link me to thine enemy. You think just because you're a married fuckin' man now that you get the moral high ground in every argument. Just ain't happening, princess." Gaine growls at me, but Kimmi steps in between us.

"Look, whether Beck fucked the totally hot and completely inappropriate woman who's now our prisoner is irrelevant." She huffs, and fluffs her hair, glancing up at the window where Tease's bright red hair stands stark against the bleakness of the dilapidated house. "Are we comfortable doing an exchange?"

"Comfortable doesn't have anything to do with it. We're getting Melissa back."

My friends exchange a look that makes my skin crawl. I grit my teeth and slam my empty beer bottle into the pavement, letting it shatter and sprinkle our boots with glass.

"Beck," Austin warns, but just like Mireya, I don't fucking listen. This goes beyond Melissa Diamond and their personal relationship with her. This is about loyalty and building a club where trust is at the forefront of everyone's minds. I honestly think my friends could learn a thing or two from Tease.

"I know y'all don't like Melissa, and I know she's been a pain in the ass, but consider this: Kent wasn't such a bad guy at first. He pulled us all out of shitty situations, and he helped us find each other. I think Mel was in love with the good in 'im. He's gone now, and she has to deal with that. It's the worst kind of punishment there is, so whatever you're thinking to try and teach her a lesson, don't bother."

"Listen," Austin begins, but I don't stop talking. I see why this situation hasn't gone any further than this. There's actually hesitation on their parts.

"You want to move forward as an MC without Kent?" I point at Austin's chest, but he doesn't back down. Good man. I'd trust him with my life, and I'm willing to risk mine for him. All I ask is that he extends the same courtesy for Melissa. "You want the Triple M'ers to trust you? Then make this your priority. It's that Musketeer shit: one for all, and all for one. We are a fucking family here, and you do *anything* for family." I pull my hand back and take a deep breath, looking around the semi-circle at the faces I know so damn well. I lost a lot of friends in my previous lives, during my time in the Army, with my previous MC. I've learned that the people you spend everyday with are the ones who mean the most, and when they don't come back, you end up spending your time pining for the impossible. "We either have each other's backs or we walk away from this right now and say goodbye to Triple M." Kimmi gasps, but neither Gaine nor Austin makes a damn peep.

"I would die without you guys," Kimmi says, and I know

she means it. I tuck my arm around her and hug her tight, wonderin' in the back of my damn mind if maybe Tease is lookin' out the window at us. "And people did die for us. We can't break up now. There aren't a whole lot of clubs that function like we do. And I am just *not* old lady material." Kimmi tries to smile, but it's a worried expression. Shouldn't be, though. I'm not trying to scare anybody shitless, just give a warning.

"I want you guys to know where I'm coming from, that's all. I think we just need to pull our shit together and maybe find somewhere to settle down." Silence descends on the group as the sun starts to set on the horizon. Even driving damn near straight, it took us most of the day to get here. I haven't even had another chance to play around with Tease. I can't stop thinking about her refusing oral sex from me. It makes me want it so much more that all I've been doing all day is formulating a plan to try and figure out how to get her to give it up to me. We did grab another burger together though. That was fun. I like the girl, a lot more than my usual take home bunny rabbits. And not just because she has round hips and creamy white thighs I could eat for damn breakfast.

"You want to settle down?" Austin asks, but the question doesn't seem fresh in his mind, more like he's been thinking about it a lot. He brushes his hand down the front of his black T-shirt, skin paling like he's damn near terrified at the thought of staying in one place for awhile.

"Doesn't have to be forever. I just think we should find a

clubhouse, have a central base of operations, somewhere to hang our hat."

"I think that's the best idea I've heard in a long fucking time," Gaine says, lighting up a cigarette and letting a hint of his New York accent shine through. Stupid fucker. I used to think he put on a Southern accent to try and please the ladies, but that's obviously not the case. Poor little pup just grew up around us idiots, and it's worn off. I almost feel sorry for him.

"We could still travel," I say, noticing that Austin is white as a damn sheet now. *What the fuck is wrong with him?* "And besides, it's just a suggestion at this point. There's a whole host of logistical bullshit we'd have to work out to even make that happen, so stop pissin' your damn pants over it." Austin shrugs my hand off when I place it on his shoulder and takes a step back.

"Alright then. Fine. Say we do an exchange. How do we work this so we don't get fucked over and hung up to dry?" I turn my gaze back towards the house and catch Tease's profile. Somehow, she starts like she senses me looking and turns to face the glass. Our eyes meet and the breath gets drawn straight out of me.

"Pick a public place, somewhere that it'd be a death sentence to start shit in." I keep looking at Tease, and I just know my friends are starting to notice our exchange. "Bring the girls there and do the switch. We can have the rest of the group waiting nearby. After that, we run like hell until we can figure this shit out. I think Tease might be right. If

Seventy-seven Brothers had wanted to plant shooters on the roof, why come and even bother to confront us? They could've put a whole host of guys up there and peppered us full of holes." I pull my gaze away with a growl. Gaine raises his eyebrow but nobody says anything.

"You got any ideas on our mystery shooter then?" Austin asks, but I got nothing for him. This isn't going to come to us in a dream; it's going to take some work.

"I don't, Pres. I got some ideas, obviously. Could be anybody from Broken Dallas or Bested by Crows, but I can't know that for certain. No worries; I'll figure it out." I light up another cigarette. At this fuckin' rate, I'm going to turn into a damn chain smoker.

"So when do we want to do this?" Kimmi asks, bumming my cig off of me and putting a hand on her hip. The chains through her belt loops jingle in the silence.

"Why not get it over with sooner rather than later?" Austin asks with a small sigh, shaking out his hands and gathering himself together. "Fuck, why drag this damn shit out another day. Let's call the bastard back and meet in the morning."

I hear the back door opening and turn to find Tease standing on the steps with Mireya at her back. True to her style, my friend's new wife has just outfitted the beautiful redhead in a pair of leather pants, some purple heels and a white tank. *Oh, fuck.*

"Not tomorrow," I say absently, my heart poundin' like a herd of fucking horses, making my chest hurt. And my crotch. Hot damn, but if my dick ain't hard as Kimmi's diamond earrings. "Make it Monday." I start to back away from the group, but Austin is giving me a weird ass look.

"Why Monday?" he asks. I know if I give him a good reason, he'll listen. But all I can think about is how I just *don't* want it to be tomorrow. I just met this girl and we're having a good fucking time. Her body is hot shit, and her mouth feels like molten fire against my mouth. I could spend all day worshippin' her skin. When I imagine letting her go, watching her walk to her brother and out of my life, I get ... weird.

Shit.

"Beck?" Austin asks again as I turn away suddenly, facing Tease in her new outfit, watching her face find mine, her expression shift to one of confusion.

"Make it Monday," I shout over my shoulder, moving towards her, ignoring the stares of my club members on either side of me. *Shit, shit, shit.* "Just trust me on this! Give me till Monday." I grab Tease by the arm and drag her against me, sliding my hand around her waist and finding her mouth with mine, tasting her breath as it mingles with my own.

She pulls away from me, eyes flicking back and forth across my face.

"What are you doing?" she asks me, grabbing a quick glance over her shoulder at Mireya's scowling face.

"Oh, don't let me stop you. Please, continue." She pushes past us and moves out into the yard as I stand there scarcely able to even believe what I'm thinking. *I do not want to walk around with a goofy smile on my face, lookin' a fool for all the world to see.* I do not want to catch what my friends have. Shoot, shit, and damn.

"Congratulations," I tell her, touching my fingers to the side of Tease's face, trailing them down her pale skin. "You're going back to your club on Monday."

"Monday?" she asks as I do my best to read her expression. This is a long shot, here, but let me tell you, I've learned my lessons in the past. When you find a good thing, you don't let it go without a fight. Not unless it wants to leave. Or I guess *she* in this matter. *So what are you even saying here, Beck?* I ask myself as Tease mulls over this information. I'm not in love. That doesn't happen for a long, long time. At least not for most people. Austin and Amy could very well be the exception to that rule. I guess all I'm saying is that tomorrow is too soon, and if I'm going to live in the moment, I want a couple more with this woman. "Did you come up with something?"

"I sure did, but it ain't what I thought it was going to be."

"I don't get it," Tease admits as I drag her up and into the house. I bet most of the rooms are full, but if we can find somewhere with a little shadow ... Hey, I'll take what I can get. I pause briefly near the front door, the hair on the back of my neck standing on end. *Not now, Goddamn it*, I think as I let go of Tease's arm and pause, cracking the door and waiting in tense silence. *Fuck me and my damn grandma.* Yup. Somethin's a comin'. "Did you hear that?"

Tease asks, and I grin.

"Sure did, sugar," I say, wrapping my fingers around her wrist and pulling her after me. She follows without protesting back into the yard, waiting behind me as I move up to Austin. Amy's brushing his sandy hair from his face, pausing to glance over at me and Tease with a smile. She doesn't know what it means when I grin this big, but Austin does. He stills her hands by touching his fingers to her wrists. "We got company, brother," I tell him, watching as he shifts from lover to leader in an instant.

"Get everyone in the house," he says, turning to Gaine and Mireya. "Take a couple people into the garage and watch the bikes, just in case. I want all the lights off and weapons in every hand." Austin spares a glance for Tease, but I meet his gaze instead.

"I got her, boss," I promise him as she turns and closes her eyes, red hair blowing in a warm gust of wind.

"Whoever that is, it's not my family," Tease promises, the sound of hogs growing louder, a growl of beasts snarling into the city and coming this way fast. If Tease says it's not her family, I believe her. This lady knows her stuff.

"I didn't think so," I tell her, watching as everyone spills into the house, weapons at the ready, faces tight with anger. We've always been a very peaceful group, but you can only push people so far before they break. I think most of my friends are at the precipice. I pity the stupid fuckers who decide to mess with us tonight. "But you know what I do think? That we have a rat. Thought that for awhile now, but it's becoming more and more obvious. Time to get out the dogs and go on a manhunt." Tease smiles sympathetically at me. "Now get your ass in the house, and let me show you how this shit is done."

"No," she says, surprising me. "I'm always in the house. I've spent my whole life in the house. If you don't mind, I'd like to stay here. I know you don't entirely trust me, but I won't do anything to compromise you. I just want to end this without anymore bloodshed."

"And I believe you, sugar, but there's no reason for you to risk yourself."

"There's a whole lot of reasons, over three hundred to be exact. That's the size of my club, all the members and their old ladies, the Mamas, the prospects. I'm fighting for them, and I've never been able to do that before."

I watch her face carefully, trying to determine where all of this strength and conviction comes from. The girl is chivalrous as all get out, and I like it. I really, really like it.

"Okay, baby," I tell her because, shoot, who the hell am I to tell her what to do anyhow? "Stay by my side and watch how it's done."

Tease
CHAPTER 17

I don't get a lot of time to wonder about Beck's strange facial expression because something happens. I don't know what it is, but I end up in the backyard of the abandoned house listening to the sound of approaching motorcycles. Whatever it is that's going on, I'm determined to be a part of it. I feel … angry right now, that strange inexplicable rage that seems to keep taking over me lately. Most of it's focused on that woman, Mireya. She's such a fucking bitch. But her clothes are exactly my style, her attitude what I'd always fantasized a woman in Triple M would be like. Tough. Outspoken. Independent. That's not to say that the women back home aren't like that at all. It's just, they all buy into this brotherhood thing where the bond between the men, their passions, their careers, all comes first. As I'd expected, it's not like that here, not at all.

I smile.

My fingers come up and touch my lips, brushing across the soft skin there. *Now all I need to do is rob a bank and I'll have had the full Triple M experience.*

"Come with me, Emilie," Beck says with a wink, drawing me along the fence and towards the narrow gate that leads into the front yard. As soon as I saw this white house towering above us, all peeling paint and spires and grimy windows, I started to fantasize about it. Who must have lived here last? Why don't they live here now? How would they feel if they knew Triple M was squatting in it? I have to shake my head and bite my lip to get rid of the thoughts. It's not easy, not with how pumped up I am. *Triple M.* I finally get to see how they work in action. *When they're not killing your family members, traitor.* I ignore that little voice in my brain, banishing it along with the fantasies. I don't blame them for that just as I don't blame Seventy-seven Brothers for killing the Triple M members. It was a costly misunderstanding, a tragic one. But blaming each other won't help. "Stay close behind me. If you need it, there's a . 38 in the back of my jeans." Beck glances over his shoulder and winks at me. "There's more than one bullet in it this time," he says with a smile, turning back to the fence and crouching low. I copy his position and wait with bated breath.

A couple of minutes slinks by, so slow that they're almost painful. I'm filled full of adrenaline, but I can't move, my legs cramping as I keep crouched beside Beck. When the noise of engines reaches a crescendo, curiosity almost kills the cat. I come *this* close to standing up. My fingers curl tight around Beck's bicep as gunshots sound in the air above us, freezing me in place. I'm used to hiding behind closed doors, hearing about the action secondhand. Right now, I'm in the thick of it, and I like the way it makes me feel.

"We know you're in there, Austin Sparks, and we're ready to raid the place 'less you get your pansy ass out here and face me like a fucking man." Beck growls low under his breath, but he doesn't move. I listen carefully in the ensuing silence and hear a slight creak and the pound of footsteps.

"I cannot for the life o' me figure out why you're here," I hear someone say. Austin, I think. I just met the man a few minutes ago, so I'm not positive on that. "Bested by Crows assaulted us, and we took care of them. I get that you have a relationship with them, but I suggest you don't involve yourself in this."

"Fucking rat," Beck whispers, his profile strong, lips sexy. I almost reach out and put my fingers on them. I have a thing for lips, especially when they're attached to a man who knows how to reach my soul with a single kiss. "I knew it. I *knew* it."

"You listen here, you crossed onto our turf without giving us the courtesy of an advanced warning, you murdered our brothers in arms, and you piss on the very idea of what an MC is all about." I can't see the man, but I know Darren wouldn't like him. He doesn't like people who preach with words. Actions are what he understands. The rest is just talk. "You mock our brotherhood by letting your bitches fly colors, ride bikes, parade around like they got bigger balls than you do."

"Did you have something to do with the shooting?" Austin asks, voice hard as steel. I decide it has to be him. He's their President, but he doesn't have a big group like we do. He doesn't have the manpower for a personal guard, doesn't have a clubhouse. It's a hands-on approach I'm not used to seeing. I think I like it. "Because this seems like an awful coincidence. How the hell did you find us anyway?"

"You owe us, so here is what we're going to do. Send your bitches out here for a beating. They're going to take it from us, and you're going to learn a lesson. We'll give 'em back to you in the morning, and then you can start paying off the monetary portion of your debt."

"Mother fuck," Beck curses. "Second time in as many days. When the shit hits the fan, it just splatters, don't it?" He holds out a hand to keep me crouching and stands up, peering out between the slats in the fence. I lean forward, bracing my fingers on the grass and trying to grab a peek, too. I can't see much, just a few men on Harleys. The leader has sunglasses on and a silver beard, wrinkled skin on his cheeks, and a nasty frown. What he's asking is downright rude. Even to Seventy-seven Brothers, who think of us ol' ladies as just bitches in the garage, we're temples. You don't hit a woman. *I wonder what Lizzie would say if she heard this*? Honestly, it'd probably give a heart attack.

"I suggest you pack your shit up and leave," Austin says, and I hear the sound of windows sliding open, hammers being pulled back. "Go home and leave us the fuck alone. If you aren't goin' to show us any respect or dignity, we don't want nothing to do you."

"Goddamn it." Beck looks down at me and winks again, touching a hand to his chest and making the sign of the cross. "Stay here and pray for me, sugar lips." He reaches down and pulls his gun out, tossing it onto the grass next to me. "I know you know how to use that thing, so don't let me down if somebody comes your way." Beck unlocks the gate and steps out, arms up in the air. "Hey y'all. Relax, brothers. We ain't got no reason to fight amongst ourselves."

"You take another step closer and we'll shoot your ass," the man with the silver beard says, examining Beck from his position on the street. *Is this what happened when Darren confronted Triple M yesterday, this same sort of scenario?* The tension is so thick in the air, I can only imagine what would happen if Beck were to explode in a spray of blood. A single shot from either side would ignite this fire, turn it into a raging inferno.

"You want to punish somebody? Make it be me."

"You? What the fuck would we want with you? Send your bitches out here and we'll let this go. All we want is to see order and tradition preserved, respected. That isn't so much to ask, is it?"

I reach out and grab the gun, holding it close to my chest as I watch Beck continue to walk forward. I'm nervous for him, my stomach twisting into knots and sweat dripping down my face. If he gets shot today, I'll never get to figure out what that look meant. It was so … sudden and unexpected. I don't like mysteries.

"Rough me up. Hell, take my life if it means so damn much to you."

"Back your ass up right now, or you're done, motherfucker," the bearded guy growls. I wonder who he is to this club. I lean forward, trying to catch the rockers on their cuts. I've never seen these guys before, and I've met a lot of groups. It must mean they're not from around here at all. They must have traveled a long, long way.

"Okay, alright," Beck says, dropping his arms and turning as if he's about to come back this way. Only he doesn't. He explodes forward in a flurry of leather and muscles, smashing into the bearded man and sending him to the pavement. I stand up suddenly and move outside the gate, raising my gun and pointing it at the men before me. I don't know who they are or why they're here, but I … don't want them to hurt Beck. He's been good to me. Really good. I swallow hard, but nobody's looking at me.

Beck is on his back on the ground, a knife up against the bearded man's throat.

"You move, and I slice the life right out o' him. So help me God, you better not bet your ass can hit me. I will warn you, I have been known to break a lot of faces." *Broken Dallas.* Those are the words written on the backs of their cuts. It's the club my brother was upset about, about Triple M disrespecting them. This goes to show there are two sides to every story. "Back up," he growls, pushing the blade into the man's skin. Red swells around the press of the knife. "Come on, on your bikes." The men of Broken Dallas exchange glances. Beck is taking a big risk here. What if these guys decide they don't care about their leader? It's happened before. *He could be killed.* I hold my breath and cock the hammer back. Gazes swing over to me and widen in surprise.

I feel so powerful standing there, like my fate is in my own hands. A lady with a gun. I lick my lips.

"You heard the man," I say, wondering where the hell this is coming from. This isn't Tease. She doesn't leave the clubhouse, doesn't do anything but show off her body, tempt the men to the edges of their sanity. That's what she does. I wonder then, if this is Emilie. My lips curl into a smile as a calmness settles around me. I could die right now. Worse could happen. But I'm okay with that. I start to see where Beck is coming from. I wonder briefly if he'll be angry with me after this is over. I'm supposed to be a hostage here, and instead, I'm standing on the front lawn of an abandoned house with a gun clutched in my fingers, defending the group that's my MC's sworn enemy. *Traitor.*

"On the bikes or he dies right here and now." Beck sits up, maneuvering the man with almost no effort, the muscles beneath his shirt sliding around, pressing against the red cotton fabric and threatening to split it wide open. I take another step forward. "I bathe in blood, baby, so I ain't scared to shed it. Get on the Goddamn bikes or I'll slice his throat for fun." The riders mount their motorcycles, but they don't look happy about it. Brotherhood. At least they really believe some of what they preach. "I'm going to wait here for awhile. You're going to ride away, and then I'll release him, just like that."

"How the fuck can we trust you?" one of the men snaps, his vest blowing in the light breeze. Beck's grin gets even wider, stretching the skin on his face.

"You can't, brother. But you're stuck between the devil and the deep blue sea, so what are you gonna do? You outnumber us two to one, so maybe you'll win. Maybe. But I'm a bit pissed off today. Sure you wanna test me, cupcake? Is some stolen pussy worth the life of your friend? You tell me that."

"Fuck you, you back country piece of shit," the man says, starting up his ride and waving his arm at his fellow club members. "Buy yourself some time now, but don't forget the clock is counting down." And then they take off, moving like a flock of birds down the narrow streets. True to his word, Beck waits in silence, still smiling, until the sound of the bikes fades away. Not a moment later, he releases the man and shoves him forward, rising to his feet and putting his boot on his back.

"Triple M might not be a big group, but it don't fuckin' matter. You know why?" The bearded men jerks away from Beck and stands up, rubbing at his throat with a scowl. "Because they got Beck fucking Evans. Get the hell out of here."

The man climbs onto his bike and leaves, dropping us into a moment of silence. And then, cheers. Whoops and calls spill out from the windows of the building as Austin climbs the remaining steps and moves over to Beck. He just happens to be sliding the bloody blade along the denim of his jeans.

"Better get the fuck out of here, Pres," he tells his friend as I lower the gun and glance around the neighborhood. Looks like most of the houses are abandoned, leaving a literal suburban ghost town populated solely with nomadic bikers. "That display of bravado is only goin' to work once."

"You crazy son of a bitch," Austin says, shaking his head and gesturing at the group with a wave of his arm. "Gonna get your ass shot one day. I swear to Christ … "

"Don't swear too hard or your grandma will spin in her grave. Let's go."

Beck gets out a cigarette and waits while the garage doors are lifted and the members of Triple M start up their rides. His eyes swing over to me, panning in almost slow motion until his gaze rests on my face.

"The gun, Evans," Austin whispers, but he doesn't need to worry about me. Beck already knows that. He walks slowly back into the yard, cig hanging from the side of his mouth, leaning over so that his voice is pouring into my ear, that slow drawl crawling into my brain and making my lashes flutter.

"Look at you, Miss Hathorne. Ain't you a peach?" And then he reaches down and takes the gun, tossing it down the hill towards Austin. "Hold that for me for a moment?" Beck asks as my thighs clench tight and my nostrils flare. *Oh God.*

"No, Beck. Goddamn it. You just said yourself, we ain't got the time."

"Won't take long," he growls around his cigarette, still grinning. I start to back up towards the yard as he stalks after me, penning me in inside the gated area. I look up at Beck's face and reach for the cigarette. His hand snatches my wrist hard and slams it against the fence boards behind us.

"What won't take long?" I ask him as he moves forward, forcing my legs apart with his knee. *Boom, boom, boom.* I can barely hear anything over the sound of my heart. That facial expression is back again, hidden under a layer of unbridled lust. I see what it is now: *interest.* Beck is interested in me. How, why, I don't know. But I like the attention.

"This," Beck says, reaching down to undo the zipper on my borrowed leather pants. They fit like a glove, making this sort of thing a hell of a lot more difficult. I should've known I was working with an expert. He slides the pants down, kicking the gate closed with his boot as he bends low, locking my ankles together in leather. When he stands up, he leans in close, cigarette smoke whirling in the air between our faces. "I can't wait to fuck you again."

"I can barely walk as it is," I whisper, but that's not entirely true. The pleasure pumping through my blood has already numbed me to any soreness down there. And I'm already wet and ready for him. My fingers come up and crawl beneath his shirt, scraping against the solid muscles there, wishing they belonged to me instead of being borrowed. I feel like I'd never get tired of touching them. My mind goes back to yesterday, to the memory of fucking him against the diner. I told myself I was doing it for survival purposes, but in reality, I think I just wanted to. Just like I do right now.

"Bullshit," he says, touching my hips and then flipping me around. I brace myself against the fence as Beck pulls my ass towards him. I try to spread my legs, but I can't, my ankles trapped in the leather like the handcuffs I wore on my wrists last night. "You're fine. It's after this that you won't be able to walk."

Beck unzips himself and pushes his dick up against me, sliding it between my cheeks, tasting the wetness with his shaft. I think of all the people outside the gate, waiting, possibly listening, but I can't keep myself quiet. Moans escape anyway.

"This is gonna be tight, babe. Brace yourself." I take a deep breath, but it doesn't prepare me for the pressure of Beck's cock as he forces it between my swollen folds, working hard to fill me up.

"It hurts Beck," I whisper as he moves inside of me, using my hips as handles, pumping slow and deep, grinding his dick against my ridges. "It hurts, it hurts, it hurts." I gasp as he slams his pelvis into my ass. It feels so much deeper like this, so much bigger. I naturally try to spread my legs again, but they're trapped. They're trapped, and I love it.

"And?" he drawls, voice wicked dark and full of masculine satisfaction. "You are so damn tight, Emilie. So tight." He continues to thrust in a slow pounding motion that makes my head spin and my knees go weak. Beck's hands on my hips are the only things keeping me upright at this point. Despite the slight bite of pain, I find myself arching my back and pressing into him. My fingers curl against the rough wood of the fence as moans drip unwanted from my lips.

"Hurry up, asshole!" one of Beck's friends shouts from the other side of the fence.

"You heard the man," Beck snarls, picking up his speed. "Hurry up before I come inside of you and decide it's time to go."

"You're so mean," I whimper because I can't think of anything else to say. Tears prick my eyes, but not out of emotion, just the sheer overwhelming sensation of pleasure, the tightness down below, the feeling of being full. I don't think I've ever felt this ... complete before. I don't think I've ever felt like this much of a *woman*. I wielded a gun and now I'm wielding a massive, throbbing cock, penetrating me so deep, it's like I can feel him in my belly. "But it feels so damn good. So good. So so so good." I cry out, my muscles quivering as I listen to Beck's snarls. My body gets even wetter, coating his dick in my natural lube, mixing my juices with his pre-ejaculate. Everything down there starts to work better, moving faster, like a well oiled machine. "Do it," I whine, hating the sound of my own voice. Wow. I just got steamrollered by Beck Evans. "Do it. Come inside."

Beck's hands tighten on my flesh, marking the same spots he bruised last night, branding me harder than any fucking jacket could ever do. *Wow, Lizzie sure would be proud of you right now. Traitor.* I ignore my inner thoughts. It's not that difficult to do with a massive cock pummeling your pussy.

Beck whoops, cheering like he's at a fucking football game or something, spilling his seed inside of me with a last violent thrust and pulling away without so much as a pat on the back. When I spin around and slam my back into the fence, he's grinning. And he already has a cigarette tucked between his lips.

Beck leans over and whispers in my ear.

"Like I said, before you go, you're getting oral sex from me. Remember this for later, and loosen up." He winks at me and bends down, grabbing my pants and sliding them up my legs, buttoning them as he presses a scalding kiss to my mouth.

I'm so horny right now, shaking with adrenaline and undeniable desperation, that I know later, if he offers, I'm going to do it. Bastard. Bastard. Bastard. I follow Beck out the gate, ignoring the catcalls and the whispers, and climb onto the back of his bike. Even angry, even quivering with pent up need, I can tell I'm going to miss this guy.

CHAPTER 18

We ride to a hotel on the outskirts of Nashville, settling in well after dark. I have all these grand plans for Tease when we get there, but she ends up falling asleep on the bike. Austin doesn't even bother to ask questions when I tell him we're rooming together. Nobody really needs to ask any questions at this point. What we were doing behind the fence is common fuckin' knowledge at this point.

"Come on, sweet thing," I whisper, lifting the girl off my bike and holding her in my arms. Nobody bothers me as I carry her to our room, laying her out flat on the bed and pulling down the covers. She stirs, but not much, making me wonder if I've somehow managed to earn her trust. I fucking kidnapped the poor girl, so I feel a little guilty about it, but it seems right somehow. *Like the hand of frigging fate reached into our lives and pushed us together.* Boy, when I saw her with that gun clutched in her hand, I almost exploded right in my fucking pants. Hottest damn shit I ever saw. "Sleep tight, Emilie," I say as I flick off the light and retreat to the patio to smoke a quick cigarette. Austin wants to meet in the bar in an hour anyway and discuss our next game plan. The whole thing makes me think of that night we went to the bar, when Gaine and Mireya picked up that girl, Crystal. How she ended up with me and Melissa instead. How Gaine found her naked on the side of the road. "Shit." I flick my smoke over the balcony and lock the doors behind me. It's a little early to go downstairs, but if Tease is asleep then I might as well go. Sitting here and having to look at her beautiful body is damn near akin to torture.

I like this girl. Just met her yesterday and I'm already interested. Like Austin was in Amy.

"I ain't ready to fall in love," I groan as I push into the hallway and pause, my gaze following the blue sign on the wall to the pool. Normally, I'd venture down there, check and see if there might be any ladies lookin' for some company. Tonight, I got Tease, and I feel good about that. Even if she is asleep. *Huh.* I shake my head and turn in the opposite direction, pausing as one of the doors on my left opens and Kimmi emerges. She's dressed in a pair of black leggings and a purple tank that displays her black bra with ease. "I like the yellow heels," I tell her as she hooks her arm around mine. "Those new?"

"I got them off a chick I banged last week." I laugh. Unapologetic, crude, just as pervy as me. That's my Kimmi.

"She left them, so I decided to keep them. As a souvenir, of course."

"You going to be able to give all that up when you fall head over heels for Christy?" Kimmi snorts and shakes her head, orange hair flying every which way.

"Like that's ever going to happen. I so much as speak to the girl and she spooks. This could be a very long process."

"But you're committed?" I ask as we move down the hallway. "I mean, you really do think you and this chick have a magic spark?" Kimmi pats my hand and grins wide, twirling her free hand around in the pearls she's got draped around her neck.

"Funny you'd be asking me that. What about the Seventy-seven Brothers bitch? You seem pretty into what she's selling." We hit the lobby, and I find myself surrounded by some sort of fancy party. A weddin' maybe? It's somehow migrated from the ballroom, into the lobby, and now over to the bar. There are bridesmaids fucking everywhere, and I'm hardly tempted. You know that whole phrase, why go out for burgers when you got steak at home? Fuck, these bitches are like McDonald's and Tease is a Goddamn filet.

"I like her, Kimmi. She's hot shit in the bedroom, and her soul is old, like she's lived a hundred lives before this one."

"Do you *feel* her though? Do you get that sense of other when you're around her? Don't think too hard about this. It shouldn't be a difficult question."

"I met her yesterday, Reynolds," I say, taking my place at the bar and ordering a whiskey sour. Kimmi orders a stout beer and we sit in silence for a minute.

"Yes, but you already feel something, don't you? There are only two ways fires can burn, Beck. One's a slow burn, a coal, an ember, that you have to feed until it grows into a raging flame. The other's an explosion. Did you have an explosion, Beck? Because since I met you, I've never seen you get that face."

"What face?" I ask, slapping a wad of cash on the bar and grabbing my drink. I toss out the cherry and the fuckin' lemon wedge and drink it down like a shot. Kimmi leans back and gives me her best *no bullshit* look.

"Like you want to own her," she says with a smirk. "Like you see something in her you've never seen in anyone else." I laugh my ass off at that one, slapping my hand on the bar and drawing curious eyes in our direction.

"Kim, would you listen to the crap that's spewing out of your throat? I don't even know how you get laid with that romance novel bull. I like the girl, and I'm interested, and sure, I'm curious. I wonder what might happen if we had more time together."

"Ah. The Monday thing makes sense now," she says with a slight smile. "But I don't know that Tease's brother is going to go for it."

"What is he going to do, tell us no? If he wants his sister back, he'll wait. I have to follow this thing through or I don't know, I'll always have that question in the back of my

C.M. Stunich

mind." I gesture loosely at the air around us, like that could explain how fucking weird I'm being right now. "When I imagine her walkin' away from me, I ... don't know. Never fucking mind."

"Hey," Gaine says, swinging onto the stool next to me. Mireya takes up the one on his right and leans her elbows on the counter. "Did I just hear what I thought I heard? And you're always making fun of me for talkin' fairytales?" I lean over the bar and give him a look.

"Ain't nobody heard nothin'," I say to him, daring him to question that shit.

"I fell in love over *years*, and I'm the overly romantic one?" Gaine asks, shaking his head and ordering a beer for him and Mireya. I don't even look over at her ass. I think the bitch is smirking at me.

"You better be talking about Austin and his little Miss Amy. Nobody said nothin' about love." I steal Gaine's drink when it comes to him and order another. "So fuck off, and shut your damn mouth."

"But you really do like this bitch?" Mireya asks, pouting her dark lips and running her tongue over the glossy lipstick she's wearing. Gaine watches her and shifts uncomfortably in his seat. Got to admit, it is kind of hot.

"I do, so I asked for a few more days, alright? Is that what you want to hear?"

"I was wondering," Austin says, coming up from behind me and putting a hand on my shoulder. Amy and Christy aren't with him, so I'm assuming he got someone else to

190

watch them for once. I don't need anybody to watch Tease. I'll know if someone tries to go up there. Trust me, I'll *know*. "Makes sense, I suppose. No more or less than me taking Amy in, but ... " He trails off and looks both excited and nervous at the same time. *Dumb shit.*

"So now everybody knows. I kidnapped this girl yesterday and today, I don't like the thought of sending her back where she damn came from. Congratulations, y'all figured it out. You want a damn ribbon?" More folks start staring at us, but they can fuck off to their fancy party.

"I'm goin' to make another phone call to Seventy-seven Brothers and discuss the arrangement," Austin says, ignoring me and taking up the stool next to Kimmi. "I found a plaza not too far from here. It's public, surrounded by shops and is supposedly pretty fuckin' busy on a Monday." He raises his blonde brows and gives me a look that I return with the finger. "Let's get this taken care of first, and then we'll deal with this all this other shit." He wipes his hands down his face. "Can you even fucking believe Broken Dallas?"

"I knew it from the first second I laid eyes on them," Gaine says, squeezing his beer bottle with rigid fingers. He looks over at Mireya, but her expression is blank. I imagine she's tired of dealing with all this gender bullshit. I know all she cares about is riding and pimping out bikes. I actually feel bad that she has to deal with all this useless crap. "They're obviously being fed information, too. We still have a rat, and it wasn't Kent. It wasn't Melissa. How the fuck else would anyone have been able to find that house? It was the perfect hiding place."

"Broken Dallas is full of hot air. We stay away from them long enough and make sure not to cross paths in the future, and they'll go away. They are a Goddamn symptom, not the fuckin' disease. Gaine is right. We need to snuff out our rat *before* we plan this exchange." I punctuate my statement with a swig of beer.

Austin twirls his cell around in his fingers and crinkles his brows together.

"How do we do that?" he asks, more to himself than to the rest of us. "We don't have a massive fucking group, but it's also not a walk in the park to investigate everybody." He leans back and sets his phone down on the bar, tapping his fingers against the dark wooden countertop. I let my eyes trail across the wall of mirrors in front of us, covered in glass shelves and filled to capacity with liquor. It's hog heaven in here, that's for sure. I order another round. A moment later, Austin stops tapping his fingers and I watch as his spine gets stiff.

"What?" Kimmi asks, turning to face him with a raised brow. "You come up with something?" We all pause in our drinking to stare at Austin and wait.

"What if they're not just feedin' information?" he asks, his brown eyes darkening. "Do y'all remember who you actually *saw* at the shoot-out?"

"I think we could all name names," Gaine says, running his hand through his dark hair. "But not everybody was there anyway. What are you getting at? You think it really was one of us that shot Melissa?"

"Could be our rat," Austin says, spinning his phone around in a circle. "Think about it. Somebody's mad about Kent, doesn't like where we're going as a group. They stay in and start feeding information to Bested, to Broken Dallas. That confrontation with Seventy-seven Brothers was like icing on the fucking cake. The more I think about it, the more sense it makes."

"Only problem is, we didn't know they were coming until they showed up. Somebody had to have time to get up on the roof like that." Kimmi makes a good point, but Mireya makes an even better one.

"When Beck came back into the restaurant, we were the only people from the club still in there." She pauses, dark eyes twinkling. I stand up from my seat because I can tell this shit is going to get ugly tonight. Mireya has an idea brewing up top. She lifts her face and smiles wickedly. "Except for one other person."

CHAPTER 19

Margot Tempe has a room on the third floor, almost directly across from mine. Just because I'm a paranoid motherfucker, I have to open my door and check in on Tease before we get down to business. When I look in on her, she's still fast asleep. I close my room door behind me and give Austin a nod.

Kimmi refused to come upstairs with us, so we left her down in the bar, biting her nails and sucking on a bright pink drink that probably tastes as nasty as it looks. Nobody wants to think their former lover's a bad guy. I think that's why Melissa's still struggling with Kent's death. It's not hard to be deceitful under someone's nose when they're in love. Love is blind, remember?

"This fucking sucks," Gaine says as he stands to the right of the door. Mireya takes up the left side, and I step forward, taking the lead. I can tell Austin wants to do it, but he's President now. He has to learn to start delegating. According to Kimmi, Margot should be alone in here, so I'm not too worried. I doubt she'll even see this coming. *If* she's our rat. The more we worked through the evidence, the more sense it makes. Kimmi does have a bad habit of pissing off the ladies.

I knock gently on the door, and wait patiently. A moment later, we hear the sound of the chain being pulled back, and then there she is, Miss Margot Tempe, smiling sexily at me. She's a little beauty, won't deny that, but I can't look at her without that cloud of suspicion hanging over her head.

"Hi Beck," she coos before noticing that I'm not alone. Her smile turns into a frown. "Is everything okay?"

"There isn't another crisis if that's what you're worried about, but we do need to have a little chitchat. Mind if we come in?" She shrugs nonchalantly and takes a step back, opening the door into the dimly lit room. The only source of light comes from the TV, and let me tell you this, those flickering shadows are a man's worst nightmare. I turn the light on right away, not that I really think Margot's hiding anyone in her room, but it doesn't hurt to be cautious. Gaine, Mireya, and I all move to the side and let Austin take over. He's getting better at it which is nice. I have no desire to be the President myself.

"Margot, mind if we talk to you for a minute about something?"

"Of course not," she says, sitting down in a pink chair

with tan polka dots all over it. "Go ahead." The girl's hair is short and dark, and she's dressed in a pair of shorts and a white tank. I can see the nipples on her itty-bitty titties through the fabric, but I'm not interested. Still caught up in Tease, wouldn't you know. Margot is so slight, I can hardly imagine her capable of riding a bike, let alone climbing a roof to shoot somebody. Then again, pretty sure she's been piggybacking around on other folks' bikes. I don't recall that she even has one of her own. And she's still wearing a prospect's jacket. I almost feel sorry for her, like the girl's been forgotten in all of the crap we been wadin' through. No excuses though. If she started this shit, she's going to have to pay.

"I'm going to ask you straight, and I'd really like it if you just told me the truth," Austin begins, laying it on her hard. "You lie to me and the consequences are going to hurt." Margot wrinkles her brow and looks between us like she has no clue what's going on. Meanwhile, I start to drift around the room, just in case I find somethin' interesting. "Did you shoot Melissa Diamond in the back?"

"Wait, *what*?" Margot asks, blinking rapidly, the pulse in her throat fluttering. I pause in my search and just stare at her. *Fuck.* The girl's as guilty as a hangman at a rope convention. It's just too damn obvious. "Of course not! How ... why are you even asking me this?"

"Kimmi's a bitch, I get it," I tell her, moving across the carpet and pausing in front of her chair. I tower over the woman, probably intimidating as hell, but that's alright. She deserves it. "Is that why you been feeding information to Bested by Crows and Broken Dallas?" Margot shakes her head.

"I've been loyal to Triple M for years," she says, which could very well be true.

"Years, but not recently," I press, stepping back when Austin gives me a look. Margot looks between me and him, letting tears build up in her eyes. It almost, *almost* makes me feel sorry for her again. I'm a sucker for women, I guess.

"Did Kimmi ask you to do this? You know, she broke up with me just on the off chance she might be able to sleep with that Christy girl." Margot shakes her head and wipes at the tears on her face. "The *off chance*. Why would she put you up to this? Why would you even do it? I'm already humiliated enough as it is."

"We're not trying to hurt you, sugar," Austin says, bending down and putting his hand on her knee. "But we want the truth. You admit it now, and you can walk away." I come *this* close to protesting, but hey, Austin's the President. It's not up to me to argue that shit. "You lie, and there are going to be other punishments, Margot. The shooter, whoever it was, got eighteen people killed unnecessarily. That is punishable by death in most circles." He pauses and strokes her hair back from her forehead. "You don't want us to find evidence that proves our point. If you really are innocent, you've got nothing to worry about. But if you're lying … " Austin trails off and stands up, looking over at me and nodding his head gently. "We'll give you some time to think about it."

He takes a step back and moves for the door handle.

"Wait," Margot begins, voice breaking on the single syllable. "Just wait. I'll tell you. I'll tell you, but you have to swear on the club that you'll let me go."

I grin wicked nasty, even though I don't mean to. Sometimes the cracked eggs are the easiest ones to break.

Tease
CHAPTER 20

I wake up the next morning with Beck lying shirtless next to me. His body is a few careful inches away from mine, but I can still feel the heat radiating from his skin, teasing me, torturing me, and reminding me that I never got to finish yesterday. I stare at him, almost afraid to wake him. If I do, he might … I can't even fucking go there without flushing from head to toe. I roll onto my back and lay my arm across my forehead. *Beck Evans. Triple M.* It's odd when a fantasy comes to life and ends up meeting your expectations. *Exceeding them even.*

I sigh and sit up, my body stiff as hell from sleeping in the corset and leather pants. At least Beck was a gentleman and left me as I was. It's already weird enough that we slept in the same bed together. I wasn't a prisoner this time, wasn't handcuffed. We were just sharing because … well, we're connected somehow now. I climb out of bed and undo the claps on the front of the bodice, peeling it away from my body with a sigh of relief and taking it into the bathroom with me. I strip off the pants next and drape both items over the toilet seat before climbing into the shower.

Part of me is desperate for Beck to wake up and come find me in here, and the other part wishes he wouldn't. *Monday.* As in the day after tomorrow. That's when I'm going back home. I feel sick inside, like I'm on a vacation that's ending too soon. I don't want to leave Beck yet, not when I still have this incredible ache inside my stomach. If he comes in here, touches me again, how am I going to pull myself away? He's the most attractive man I've ever seen in my entire life. I don't envy trying to search for someone that lives up to him.

"Crap," I lay my forehead against the glass door of the shower and sigh heavily. And he's interested in me. *Interested.* I'm not exactly clear on what that means, but I'd like to find out. "Crap, crap, crap." I finish up my shower quickly, determined to be done before Beck finds me, soapy and scalding hot.

Unconsciously, I start to move a little bit slower.

Holding back that orgasm yesterday has lit this slow burning fire in my lower parts. Even walking into the bathroom, I could feel my body rubbing, practically begging me to touch it. I haven't though. Not that I've got anything against masturbating, but Beck is here and willing ... Or at least he would be if he wasn't still sleeping.

I climb out of the shower to find him in bed, same

position I left him. *Damn it.* I don't feel like we're on close enough terms that I could just go and wake him up for sex. I know realistically that he probably wouldn't mind, but it still seems weird. As I'm moving back down the short hallway to the bathroom, somebody grabs me from behind. My heart flutters in panic before I realize those scalding fingers burning against my flesh belong to Beck.

"I thought you were sleeping," I say as he pulls me back into the room and flings me on the bed, my white towel fluttering like a broken angel wing. I do my best to cover up my nakedness while Beck stands over me grinning.

"I was waitin' for your ass, sugar tits."

"I like it best when you call me Emilie," I tell him honestly and his grin morphs into a more gentle smile. "Not that it really matters."

"Oh, it matters alright," he says, stripping his jeans off and letting them fall to the floor. Beck doesn't seem to have the same problem I do with flashing his naked body around. His cock is already hard and glistening with sweat. I don't know what it is about these fucking hotel rooms, but this one is just as warm as the last one, drenching Beck's entire muscular frame in little beads of moisture. I bite my lower lip as feelings surge deep within my belly. *Oh my God.* The man is built like a God, a statue chiseled in living flesh. His pecs are rock solid but not grotesquely oversized, tapering into a perfect belly with an eight pack and that incredibly irresistible 'V' shape of his oblique muscles. His thighs are thick without being beefy, much like his arms with that perfect swell of shoulder and bicep. And the tattoos? There's the pirate symbol, the skull and crossbones on his chest with the 'MMM' above it.

I reach up a hand and run my fingers through my wet hair, trying to still my rapid breathing. I feel like I'm *this* close to panting at the man.

"I want to call you what makes you hottest, darlin'. If it's Emilie you like, Emilie it is."

"What were you waiting for?" I ask him, even though I already know. He grins at me and moves forward, kneeling on the end of the bed and reaching out for the towel. I try to keep hold of it, but Beck's a hell of a lot stronger than me. It goes fluttering through the air and lands in a heap on the floor. Leaving me naked. Leaving me exposed. I put my hands over the spot of red hair between my legs. "I was in the shower that whole time."

Beck crawls forward and drapes his naked body over mine, burning me his nearness, making me gasp even though he isn't touching me.

"Absence makes the heart grow fonder," he growls into my ear, drawing back and pushing my knees apart. "Tell me you don't feel this, Emilie." He presses a hand to my belly, rekindling that burn into a fire. Absently, I remember that we haven't used a single condom. Not one. I look up at Beck and find that I'm having a hard time breathing. I could ask him to use one now, but ... I don't want him to. I want to feel his body bare against mine. Now that I've had it, I'm feeling selfish. I don't want a piece of latex separating us.

Shit. Future Tease is going to have problems. Present Tease is living in the moment with Beck Evans and couldn't give a shit less.

"Feel what?" My voice is a whisper as I watch him lower himself, sliding his arms under my thighs and reaching around them, using my hips as handles again. I'm going to be so, so sore there come Monday. I lean my head back into the pillow and relax my arms. I'm still not entirely comfortable with this, but he's wooed me into it, denying me yesterday, teasing me today. I just need *something* from him, and this is going to be it. I reach my hands up and grab onto the headboard.

"The explosion," he whispers against my pussy, his breath alone causing me to gasp and buck my hips. *What if he's staring at it*? *Nobody's seen that, not even me. What the fuck am I thinking*? But then Beck's lips press gently against my folds and I collapse into the bed, spine going limp, muscles turning to jelly. I groan so loud I'm sure the people in the next room can hear us. He starts out slow, kissing me gently down there, pressing his mouth to my inner thighs, my knees, and then working his way back until he lands on my clit. "The fuckin' magic," he says, his words a physical force against my body, his breath teasing me to the point of tears.

"Fuck me," I whisper, trying not to sound like I'm begging for it. But I kind of am, so that's okay. "Just fuck me." Beck laughs, and I almost scream. It feels so good it's almost painful.

"Not yet. I told you, you ain't gettin' out of here without tasting all the flavors, honey." More words, more breath, followed by more kisses. I bite my lower lip so hard it bleeds. His warm tongue invades me now, sliding up along the crease between my legs, finding my clit and moving gently over it, like a feather.

"Fuck," I moan, squeezing my hands even tighter around the wood spindles. "Fuck, Beck. Stop. I can't do this."

"You can, and you will," he tells me in a deep rumble, flicking his tongue a little harder against my clit. "And you'll love every damn second of it." His finger finds my opening, pushing inside, giving me a taste of what I want but stopping short of the real thing. It's maddening. I just want that feeling of fullness, of completeness, of being joined with another human being for a perfect moment in time.

"I want it," I growl at him, but he doesn't stop. He keeps kissing me, alternating hard flicks of his tongue with the soft, gentle press of his lips. "I want it now." Beck thrusts his finger inside of me again, moving in a gentle rocking rhythm. Slowly, he inserts a second, taking away a bit of the pressure but not enough. My spine feels tight, like it's curling from the buildup, twisting inside of me until I want to thrash and scream. "Beck," I whimper, dropping my hands down and tangling them in his hair, pulling hard and trying to get him to come up to me.

The man doesn't budge.

Instead, he puts a third finger inside of me and sucks the hard bud of my clit gently into his mouth.

"*Ah*, please stop," I whisper, my voice close to breaking. "Please stop. Beck, *please*." He ignores me, scraping his teeth gently along the most sensitive part on my fucking body. I do scream then, bucking my hips hard and coming up against firm resistance. Beck won't let me move. I yank at his hair and thrash, but I can't get him to budge. "Beck, no!" I scream as he continues to move his fingers in and out, slowly but surely, his mouth sucking on my clit with a firm but gentle pressure. "Beck!" This last one comes out in a screech and them I'm throwing my head back into the pillows and groaning like the air's just been knocked from my lungs. Unintelligible sounds scrape from my throat and drown me until I collapse into a near weeping puddle. The orgasm was good, but it wasn't enough. Not enough. "Beck," I whisper as he chuckles against my body and plants one, last kiss on my clit. His fingers slide out, leaving me empty and desperate for it.

"At your fuckin' service," he growls, sliding his body up mine, touching his wet fingers to my left breast and massaging it with a firm grip before dropping his mouth to my pert nipple, standing up like a pink soldier at attention. I arc my hips against him, begging for it with my body. I don't think I can take anymore. I'm not used to this heat, this passion. I have *never* in my life even come close to experiencing the depth of feeling I've got going on right now. Beck is stirring my apathetic soul awake.

And I only have one more day after this to share with him.

"Hurry Beck," I whisper into his ear, scraping my teeth along his earlobe. "Do it. Fuck me." He chuckles against my breast and kisses his way up to my mouth, capturing my lips with that soul gripping intensity, that fire, the slick brush of his tongue. Our mouths dance together as he adjusts himself down below and strokes his dick along the wetness. It's extra slippery with his saliva, making it really easy for him to find my sweet spot and slide in deep.

"Oh, Emilie," he grunts as our pelvises make contact, naked bodies pressed tightly together. "Oh, baby." Beck puts his elbows on either side of my head and looks down at me. "You feel so fucking good." He moves inside my heat, rocking his body to my rhythm as I raise my hips to meet him, trying to make sure I get every inch, not caring if I'm being greedy or not. I lock my ankles behind his ass, pulling him tighter into me until his balls are being crushed against my cheeks. I put so much pressure on him that he stops thrusting and instead just rocks his hips into mine, clashing our bodies together at the spot where we meet. The movement rubs my clit in just the right way, drawing sweat from my forehead that drips down and soaks the pillow. My eyes go blurry again and I find myself coming, not once or twice but three fucking times. Layers of pleasure stack on top of one another, weighing me down, crushing the air from my lungs and drawing one last scream from my throat. Beck times his release with mine, grabbing my head between his hands and kissing my mouth so hard our teeth clash as he comes inside of me, marking me, claiming me, making me wish I never had to leave.

Tease
CHAPTER 21

After we finish fucking, I fall asleep again and wake up angry with myself for wasting time with Beck. *Since when did time with this stranger become such a precious fucking commodity?* When I open my eyes fully, I find him sitting on a chair and lacing up his boots.

"Good afternoon, Emilie Hathorne," he says, standing up and moving over to the edge of the bed. I roll onto my back, keeping the sheet over my breasts to hide my nipples from him. They're rock hard and already ready for another round. Me, I'm not so sure I could take it again. The area between my thighs is sweetly sore. And sticky. Very, very sticky. Beck leans down and presses a kiss to my forehead that surprises the hell out of me. I did not expect that one. A hot fuck, sure. A sweet and gentle kiss? I shiver. "If you wouldn't mind getting dressed, I've got something I want to talk to you about."

I sit up abruptly.

"What?" The word sounds harsher than I mean it to, but I can't help myself. No good conversation has ever started out with those words. "Did something happen to my family?" Beck pauses and then bites at his lip.

"You sure you don't want to get dressed first?" he asks, freaking me the fuck out. I shake my head and sit back against the headboard, heart pounding a million miles a minute.

"Please just tell me before I have a heart attack." Beck sighs and rubs at his red hair, sitting down on the edge of the bed next to me.

"It isn't all sunshine and roses, Tease. But it's nothing you need to have a panic attack over." Beck pauses. "I don't think." I stare at him, refusing to draw my gaze away from his eyes until he tells me what this is about. I don't like mysteries. Beck watches me carefully and then sighs, nodding his chin and sitting up straight. "I want to be honest with you, Tease." He pauses. "Emilie. I've got to tell you this before somebody else does." I put my hand on my chest and close my eyes, waiting for the other shoe to drop. "We found the shooter." Chills crawl up my spine, and my eyes snap open.

"Who?" I can't take the anticipation, cannot even fucking stand it. This has to solve things, doesn't it? I know I'm grasping at straws now. This has changed from a mission of morality and trying to protect my family, to somehow wishing and hoping and praying that our clubs will get along. That it'll be okay for Beck and I to speak with each other. See each other. Maybe.

I think my eighteen years are showing. Beck is *interested*, but he never implied even once that he'd want a relationship with me. I'm probably too young for him anyway. Or he's too old for me.

I put my hands over my face.

"It was a girl in our club, Emilie. A rat, a traitor, yes, but a Triple M'er." My heart sinks to the floor. "Her name is Margot Tempe, and while I wish I could curb stomp her ass, my Pres won't let me. He wants to release her and then pass the information to your brother, let him do what he deems appropriate." I swallow hard. What Darren deems appropriate probably wouldn't sit well with these people. There's a very good chance Margot won't live to see another birthday. "We want you to make the call, confirm the arrangements of the trade with him, and see what he says."

"That's probably a good idea," I whisper, knowing exactly what my brother is going to do and say. He'll accept the terms, and he might, *might* let Triple M walk for giving up Margot. That'll be the extent of his generosity. "But that's not all you have to tell me, is it?" I can sense more – worse things even.

Beck sighs again and adjusts himself, leaning his elbows on his knees.

"Can I tell you a story, Emilie?" he asks me, and I nod. I have a crush on the man. That much is painfully obvious. I'm already at the point where I'll listen to any story he wants to tell me. "It won't excuse what I've done, but it might help you understand it." Beck closes his eyes for a moment, like he's gathering himself together. When he opens them again, they look even greener than they were before, even though I know that isn't possible. "Okay, here goes." Another deep breath. "I was a good kid, Emilie. I had a mom and a dad and we were alright. My dad was strict, and my mother followed his orders like a soldier. But they loved me best they could, so I did what they wanted me to do and joined the Army." He raises up his hands, flashing me the word *Hopeless* again. It's a weird word to see on this man's knuckles. From my experience being around him, he seems anything but hopeless. "I won't bore you with war stories, but it fucked me up good, and I ended up losing a lot of people that I cared about." Beck looks down at his intertwined knuckles. "I failed a psych test and was discharged. After that, I was so messed up that I just wandered until I found somewhere I could belong. That was important to me after being in the military. I wanted a group, a brotherhood. I ended up in an MC that ain't worth the shit on my boots, and I did bad things. I hurt people that maybe didn't deserve to be hurt. And the only reason, the *only* reason I escaped that life was because Triple M found me and gave me a new place to belong, a new family to believe in."

"Beck," I whisper, but I'm not sure where he's going with this, so I try to keep quiet. He closes his eyes and keeps talking, like if he stops he might not be able to start up again.

"When somebody hurts or threatens that family, I get a little crazy. I won't lie to you about that."

"I understand," I tell him, because I do. This is one of the few things in life that I actually get.

"And when that shot went off and Melissa went down, I lost my shit. I shot at least three of your club members." I swallow my pain and close my eyes, too, like if I can't see his face, it'll make it less real. Watching Beck, I could tell he was a badass. Of course he killed some of my family members. Of course he did. But I can still pretend, right? As long as I don't know who exactly he murdered. But Beck's not done. "And I stabbed one of them, several times. The man with the blue eyes, the Sergeant at arms."

"Oren," I whisper and I don't know whether to feel angry or ... relieved. *Traitor.* No, no, I'm angry. I *knew* Oren. We had dinner together in the club room, played pool. He watched over me, and just because I didn't want to be his old lady, I can't tarnish his memory. I have to be respectful. He was family, family, *fucking family.* Beck adjusts himself and I open my eyes, staring into his and wanting so much to forgive but not knowing how. I can't forgive him, not me alone. The club has to forgive him and that is never, never, *never* going to happen.

"Tease," Beck whispers, and I can tell there's something else he wants to say to me. But I'm not ready. Might not ever be ready. Even though I want to be. Even though I want him so bad it hurts. I shouldn't, but I do. Whatever it is he wants to say, I don't want to hear it. If I do … Traitor will be the nicest word in the book for me.

"Would you mind looking away, so I can grab my clothes?" I ask and Beck nods, face falling, that omnipresent grin disappearing like a seashell in the ocean. I reach over and cup my hands around his. *Live in the moment.* I still have a few days to spend with him, so that's what I'm going to do. I'm going to enjoy myself and then I'm going to walk away. Because that's the right thing to do. It's what Darren, what Seventy-seven Brothers, would want from me. I can't sacrifice everything for a man I just met, who I don't have the capacity to forgive. "I'll get dressed and make that phone call." I pause and glance away. "And then, maybe, we could find something to do together?" I look back at him and try to smile. I'm being ridiculous – it's impossible to feel this much for a stranger. Impossible. "I could always go for another hamburger."

CHAPTER 22

Letting go of Margot Tempe is not an easy thing for me to do. When I look at her face, all I see are the ones we lost in the shoot-out. I clench my hands at my sides and sneak a furtive glance around the group. Triple M ain't happy either, but I think if they look at it from Austin's point of view, they'll see that this is the best possible solution. We let Margot walk, show sympathy to our fallen sister, and she stumbles straight into the hands of Seventy-seven Brothers. She'll get her just desserts, and we'll have shown mercy. Seventy-seven Brothers will take our straight trade, and we can walk away from this, grieve, and move the fuck on.

'Cept I'll still be thinkin' of Tease long after she's gone. It's gonna take a whole truckload of beautiful bunnies to forget this woman. Goddamn you, Emilie. I can't have a girl waltzin' into my life and turnin' it upside down, just isn't me. You know, this afternoon when I went downstairs for a

smoke break with Kimmi, I actually stopped to smell some roses. Like fuckin' literally. I sniffed the damn things.

I touch a hand to my forehead and smoke my cigarette, glancing over at Tease. She's been acting weird since I gave her my stupid ass speech. I've been rehearsing the damn thing since she fell asleep, fighting myself on whether I should even bring that crap up. But I gave myself the weekend to test this out, so that's what I'm going to do. She has to know about me, all the dirty truths. I won't admit to myself *why* I need her to know. Why I'm trying to stuff a life altering revelation into a couple o' days. I'm not even sure what I want to happen after all this. Say Tease and I get along, have a good time, then what? She stays in Triple M? The thought really ain't all that far-fetched if you think about it.

The doors to the hotel open, and my attention shifts to Margot in her jeans and her orange tank top. She has her duffel bag hanging off one shoulder, and her Triple M jacket draped over one arm. As soon as she emerges outside, the hisses start up, the insults, the name-callin'. I feel violence boiling all around us, threatening to break free. If that happens, even my Beck bullshit won't be able to save Miss Margot.

"Thank you for your sympathy," Margot says to Austin, but his face is stoic, frozen into a blank expression. I have no idea what he's feeling right now. I sure hope Amy does because that man is going to need all the support we can give him. She hands him the jacket and he takes it, stepping aside as Margot makes the walk of shame, head down, eyes on the pavement. Kimmi refused to come down here, deciding to sit in her room instead. I wonder if she's watching on the balcony? I glance up but don't see her. *Damn it Margot. Fuck you Mint.* Why can't poor fucking Kimmi get a break?

Austin turns to look at Tease, and my attention shifts to her back, draped in property patches. Without hesitation, she moves forward and takes Austin's cell from his hand. The group grows quiet while she dials the number.

"Tax?" she asks and then pauses, looking out over the sun soaked pavement towards the road where Margot's heading with her bag. "Triple M's identified the shooter as one of their own." She takes a step back, red hair billowing around her face. A moment later, she glances over her shoulder and meets my eyes. I smile at her, even though this isn't the happiest fuckin' party I ever been to. "Her name is Margot Tempe, and they're willing to release her to you. She'll be at the 5th Avenue bus station in Nashville by three o'clock." Tease keeps watching me. I'm sure the whole of Triple M is wondering what's going on between us right now. I hope finding out Margot was the shooter will cool their jets a bit. I don't want any of that anger taken out on Tease. "And they accept your terms. We'll exchange at the Grand Bent Plaza Monday at noon." Tease turns away from me and hands the phone to Austin.

He takes it and from her and reconfirms the information. Provided Margot doesn't run for it and actually uses that bus ticket we bought her, we might be able to appease Seventy-seven Brothers. If she doesn't, well, at least we'll have given her a chance to escape. Not that she deserves it, but hey, mercy is an underrated trait anyhow. I move forward, breaking away from the crowd and pausing behind Tease.

"The plaza then," Austin says looking at Tease and then up at me. "I hope we can trust Tax not to screw us over?" he asks, and she needs nod.

"Melissa?" I ask because I haven't heard a damn word about her injuries. Tease turns to face me, tucking her hands into the pockets of the jeans she borrowed from Mireya. Paired with the red tank, the jacket, the purple heels … fuck me down to the border and back. I know Tease suggested we go out for burgers again, but maybe I'd rather stay in and have something else to eat. That body is makin' my damn stomach rumble.

"My brother said she was fine, and if there's anything about him to be admired, it's his honesty. You'll get what he says you'll get." She smiles at me and tucks some of her hair behind one ear. I like how she wears it, down, parted slightly to the side. Nice and casual, no thrills. It's so fucking sexy, I lift my hand up and run my fingers through it. Tease closes her eyes and leans her head into my hand, drawing a deep exhalation of breath from my lungs. When she realizes what she's doing, she opens her eyes and steps away abruptly. "Thank you for thinking about what I said, for digging beyond the obvious. It doesn't seem like much, but finding out who shot your friend and why, this is a big

217

deal to the club. It's going to make all the difference in how this turns out. And as far as Broken Dallas goes, I'll talk to my brother about them. He could pressure them to back off." Austin narrows his eyes like he doesn't trust Tease, but I give him a look. He might be my President, but he's also my friend and he knows when to back off. Hell, he should be thanking the stars that Tease is around – I haven't checked out Amy's ass since I met her.

"We'll take care of our business, but thank you," Austin says, looking back at the club as they start to disperse. Nobody crosses the curb and leaves the area of the parking lot. Austin told them if they did, they may as well leave and never come back. That, and the promised I'd break their faces in. He doesn't want anybody going vigilante on Margot. I watch as he gets out a cigarette. "I guess we have some free time?" Austin shakes his head. "Though I don't know how I'm ever going to enjoy it. Don't think I could relax again, not after what happened in Korbin." He looks up at me and we exchange a glance. "I guess I could look into this clubhouse shit." I whoop at him and cause poor little Miss Amy to jump as she approaches us. I toss her a wink and a grin and grab Tease around the waist. I don't really mean to do it, just happens. Casual touching. First sign you been bit by the bee and are about to drown in honey.

"Clubhouse?" she asks, pausing next to us and looking at Tease with interest. That's a good sign in my opinion. Amy seems to have a knack with other women. I watched her with Mireya at the pool a while back, watched her damn near charm the pants off the bitch. Hell, she even got both Mireya and Melissa to read her fuckin' romance novels. If she likes Tease, then I think I'm on the right track here. Makes me feel like less of a pussy fairytale reading bitch – like Gaine.

"No promises, sugar," he says, smiling around his cigarette. "Just an idea. Personally, I can't imagine life stuck in one place, but … I'm starting to see the advantages. A fucking chance to breathe being one of them." Tease smiles that magnetic little half-smile, and my fingers tighten on her flesh.

"Darren – " Tease starts to talk and then stops abruptly. "*Tax*," she corrects herself. "Is hardly ever at the clubhouse except for church and a get-together once a month." She stops talking and takes a deep breath, her eyes going blank for a moment, like she's not sure if she's even supposed to be saying this. Tease blinks her eyes to clear them. "I wouldn't worry about getting stuck there. Eventually, you'll just be praying for a couple nights in a row."

"That right?" Austin asks, giving her a strange look and then lifting his eyes to mine. I raise my brows and then shrug. We've been bachelors forever together, hunting girls down with Kimmi while Gaine tagged along in the background, pretending he didn't give a fuck about Mireya. And in the span of what, a friggin' month, we're dropping like flies? Shoot, son.

"If the girl says so, it must be God's honest truth." I grin.

"My momma taught me that. A real man never questions a lady." I tip a pretend hat to my friends. "Now if you'll excuse us, we got burgers to grab."

Tease
CHAPTER 23

The meeting is set. Monday. I don't know that I've ever looked forward to a date with such trepidation. And that girl, Margot … I want to call my brother and beg for her life. She just looked so … trapped. I can relate to that. I know he won't be wickedly cruel, but I doubt he'll spare her life either. The whole thing is just sad. I think of Oren and glance over at Beck, at his hands, those fingers carved with the word *Hopeless*, and I imagine him thrusting a knife into Oren's body.

"I want to forgive you, you know," I tell Beck as we start down a trail that begins near the back doors of the hotel. Behind the building, there's a whole sweep of wild forest with dirt trails winding through it. I found advertisement for it in the box at the front counter. It seemed as good as anything for what I'm starting to feel like is a first date. A first date with someone I already had sex with. Multiple times.

"Yeah?" Beck asks, not bothering to ask what about. He knows. I know he knows. I sigh and twist my fingers together, trying to find the right words. *Swept away, kidnapped, burned.* My time with Beck has been a whirlwind of activity and probably the wildest couple of days in my entire life.

"For Oren, for the others. But I can't. Only the club can forgive you, and they won't. For a long time, if ever." Beck is nodding, glancing up at the trees and the speckled spots of sunshine.

"That's alright, Emilie. I get it. I understand you got your loyalties, same way I got mine." He looks over at me and winks. I smile back. "So don't worry about that. I'm just glad you're still talkin' to me." He reaches up and laces his fingers together behind his head. "And I'm sorry to lay all that heavy shit on ya, but I wanted you to know." I don't ask him why. I can't know that. I can't hear him say something I'm only thinking in the back of my head. *Could we work together? Even though we just met? Even though I'm eighteen and he's thirty? That he's from Triple M and I'm from Seventy-seven Brothers?*

"Thanks for the hamburger," I tell him, garncring another laugh. The sound is muffled in the trees, but pleasant. It's nice out here, peaceful. "And tell Gaine thanks for the ... badger story." Beck full on chortles at that one, pausing to bend over and put his hands on his knees. "Way too much information, but it was interesting. I'm still having trouble figuring out how the badger got into the gym in the first place."

"Stick around awhile and he's sure to tell it again. You'll get the full story eventually."

"I don't know that I want the full story," I say as Beck stands up and we continue our walk. The urge to reach over and grab his hand is overwhelming. I feel like a teenager again. What thirty year old biker wants to walk around a forest holding hands? "And thanks for coming on this walk with me. I can't imagine it's something you do often."

"Shit, sugar lips, this is the best day I've had in years. And not just because of the sex." He raises his brows at me, and I meet his gaze, remembering the feel of his lips down there. It truly makes me question why I waited so long to try oral sex out. Given, I doubt either of my previous boyfriends could've won me over like Beck. He went down on me like he kisses – hot, searing, stabbing straight into my soul. They might've just drooled all over down there and scarred me for life. I shiver. "And you're right. I don't do shit like this often. Hell, I don't do shit like this ever. I drink, party, and screw around. I beat the crap out of people and I ride my bike. That's about it. I ain't all that interesting." I bite my tongue to stop myself from blurting out: *you're interesting to me.*

"Neither am I. The hardest part of my day is choosing which set of heels to wear or what shade of lipstick to apply. I hang out at the clubhouse on Tax's good graces, just waiting for somebody to snatch me up as their old lady." I breathe in, out. I can feel Beck's gaze burning into the back of my neck as I stare down at the purple heels, so out of place against the dirt trail. "Even though I don't want any of them to. I feel like I'm on borrowed time, that someday soon, Tax will just give me away."

"So why stay?" Beck asks, and I cringe because that's a loaded question that I don't even know how to answer. I love my brother. I love my club. I belong. It sounds so hollow in my head that I don't bother to say it aloud.

"My sister didn't," I tell him instead, looking up and finding myself at a crossroads. *How fucking poetic.* I glance down one side and find a couple making out on a rock. Nobody from the club, just some teenagers, probably around my age. I wonder how they ended up here together, what their parents think of their relationship, if they even care. Beck decides on our path for us and starts down the right fork. "As soon as she could, she left the club, my brother, and me behind. Since I turned eighteen, she's been coming around, trying to convince me to leave, but I don't know. I don't think I'm cut out for the real world."

"Doesn't get any realer than this," Beck says with a whistle and another grin. "You can cut it here, you can cut it anywhere. But I get where you're coming from. That's why I'm trying so hard to preserve Triple M. This is where I'm meant to be. Second I met the folks in the club, I knew." We walk for a little while in silence before he adds, "We're here for the folks too fucked up for society, too fragile for anywhere else on earth. Guess you could just say we serve a niche market." I smile, too widely maybe. Whether he knows it or not, he's really, really tempting me. *Traitor.*

"Motorcycles, madness, money. I like the whole Triple M thing. I guess you know where our club got its name? That my brother always rides out with seventy-seven men?"

"I've heard the rumors," Beck says, green eyes catching the light and shimmering. "But I didn't believe it until I saw it. Impressive set-up your brother's got going there. I'll give him that."

"He's driven, that's for sure. He knows what he wants, and he works hard to spread his beliefs." I sigh. "*Should the Need Arise.* He put that on the back of the club's jackets after my father passed away, and he was voted in. Darren … " *Damn it.* "Tax believes in family first. Respect second. Dignity, honesty, and pride. If he thinks those things are missing somewhere, that's where he goes. Where the need is. I guess he was trying to teach you all a lesson." I hang my head, but Beck mistakes it for shame, touching my chin and raising my face to his. I can't take my eyes off his lips, standing there on the path like I've been rooted in place.

"You're a good woman, Tease. And you come from a good family, I see that. But you're you. Not your brother, not your club. They're your family, but they can't define who you are or control you, not if you don't want them to. The best way for us to connect with the folks in our lives is to find ourselves first." And then he leans over and kisses me, tongue sliding between my lips, hand curling around my waist. We stand there, just kissing for several moments, the sunshine dappling our faces, before we hear laughter.

I pull away suddenly and find the two teenagers from earlier moving down the path away from us. I smile.

"You've got to stop doing that or ... "

"Or you'll fuck me again?" I glance up sharply at his face, at the laugh lines near his eyes, his red hair. "Then I guess I better keep going." Beck pulls me closer again and leans his face down, breathing hot breath across my cheeks.

"This is getting risky, Beck. We haven't used a condom even once." He pauses.

"I'm clean. Don't tell me a girl as tight as you isn't?" He tries to make it a joke, but it isn't, not really. I let him touch my neck with his fingers, back me up against a tree. *Crap, Tease! Not again.*

"I'm sore, Beck," I groan as he kisses my neck and lifts my left thigh up with one hand, spreading me open against him. Even through our jeans, I can feel the bulge in his pants. "I could get pregnant." This gives him a moment of pause at least.

"You're not on birth control?" he asks, sounding like maybe this is the first time he's thought to wonder about this. I touch my hands to his chest, press my palms against his solidness, his strength. I love that about him, love the idea that he could protect me no matter what, fight for me. If he wanted to, that is. But I like the fantasy of it regardless. "Well, sugar, you should've said something." He reaches down with his right hand and unzips his pants, exposing his cock right there in the middle of the trail. If those teenagers come back, they're going to get an eyeful. "But I still don't regret it. If anything happens, you just tell me what you want me to do. Whether you're here or back at your clubhouse, you call me." I don't tell him that Darren would never allow that. If I did get pregnant, the baby would be raised in the club, just like I was. Beck would never know.

"What if I can't?" I ask him as he pushes my pants down my hips and uses his boot to drag them to the forest floor. It's an effective way of getting the jeans off *quick*. Beck releases my thigh and sets my foot on the ground, bending down and pulling off my borrowed heels, chucking them to the side before he stands up and puts his hands on either side of my face. I stand there, my bottom half buck naked, pressed against the rough bark of the tree. Surreptitiously, I use my right foot to pull my left leg completely out of the jeans.

"Then stay," Beck says, sending chills down my spine. "If you're worried, stay. I mean, it's a long shot, but if you like Triple M then give it a chance." He touches his hand to my cheek and leans in, kissing the side of my mouth.

"Are you saying that in case I *am* pregnant?" I ask. I feel like I need clarification. Right now. It's stupid, but I want to hear him say he likes me, that *he* wants me to stay. Maybe it's because I'm eighteen and inexperienced or maybe it's just because I have that desperate need to belong. "I doubt I am, but … I don't want you to feel obligated on the off chance that it happens." Beck presses something into my hand – a condom. I squeeze it tight and then end up opening my fingers and letting it fall to the forest floor. "Because the club would take care of me. Nobody else has to."

"Nobody else has to, but if someone wanted to?" I reach down and grab Beck's cock as his hand lifts my thigh again, guiding him to my opening with a sigh of relief. Even though I'm sore, I want it. I *need* it.

"Who?" I ask, but Beck doesn't answer, thrusting into me with a grunt, grinding my bare ass against the tree. My question hangs in the air, just half a phrase, an idea. *Who would want to*? I do. That's the real answer. I want to take care of *myself*. I just need to figure out the best way to do that. *Traitor*.

"I won't lie to you, Tease. The risk turns me on." Beck growls into my ear, pushing inside of me again and again, letting his grunts ring out alongside my moans. If anyone else had the bright idea to take a walk today, I'm sure we've just ruined their afternoon. Beck doesn't bother to kiss me this time, so I wrap my arms around his neck and bury my face against his chest, letting him fuck me as hard and fast as he wants to. I nip at his skin, sliding my teeth across his flesh as my mind roils and I wonder what the fuck I'm doing here. Why I'm waiting until Monday to see my brother. I'm not a captive anymore, not really. I could've asked to go back sooner. And Beck would've let me. So why. Why. Why. Why am I staying, and why does he want me to stay?

"Me, too," I whisper back, raising my chin and looking straight into his eyes, getting lost in green as my face flushes and my nipples harden. I don't want to get pregnant, and I'm pretty doubtful that I will, but it really makes me think about my life and how I want to live it. When I imagine raising a baby in the club, I feel sick. "Me, too, Beck."

"I'm goin' to come inside of you, baby. Shoot my seed straight up into your womb." I groan as Beck's hand grabs my ass and pulls me closer. He nips my lip and breathes his beautiful Southern drawl against my mouth. "I'm gonna fuck you so hard, you end up with twins."

"Do it," I whimper at him, melting again, turning into a boneless puddle of flesh and pleasure. Beck is like a drug, and I'm thoroughly addicted. "Do it. Do it now." He grunts again, a deep animalistic sound of pure male pleasure tearing from his throat. I let my eyes flutter closed and give into the addiction.

CHAPTER 24

I'm sitting at the bar, real late, drinking a beer with Austin, Gaine, and Kimmi. Mireya's at the pool with Christy and Amy, but not because anyone told her, too. She went *willingly*. This is a big fucking step for that woman. I don't think in all the time I've known her that she's ever had a single female friend.

"Hey Austin," I ask nonchalantly, spinning my bottle in a circle on the bar top. "What would you do if you got Amy pregnant?"

"The fuck?" Austin says, getting way too friggin' excited for his own good. I give him a look and a raised brow. "Why on God's green earth would you ask me that?"

"Real question here is, what are you so afraid of?" Gaine asks him, steerin' the conversation in a completely different direction than I'd intended. I try not to groan, and sit back with my drink, exchanging a look with Kimmi.

"I ain't afraid of shit," Austin says, sitting back down and glaring at me like this is all my friggin' fault. He pauses and his nostrils flare. "Not a damn thing."

"Not even the idea of settling down into a clubhouse?" Kimmi prods, leaning forward and putting her elbow on the bar. "Because as soon as I came back to you with a perfectly affordable and *available* option, you flipped out."

"You mean, I told you to get lost because my pants were halfway down my hips and I was *this* close to bangin' Miss Amy. Next time you knock on my door and tell me it's an emergency, there better damn well be one." Kimmi grins, but she doesn't apologize. Meanwhile, I'm fuckin' sitting here thinking about Tease and trying to decide what I should do, if I should just come right out and say it to her face. *I want you to stay.* I down the last of my beer and set the bottle on the counter, running my hands down my face. This is gettin' complicated up in here. The more I think about sending her back to Seventy-seven Brothers and imagine her becoming somebody's ol' lady, the more I flip the fuck out. And now I find out she ain't on birth control? Shoot.

"I'm goin' upstairs. If you need me, I'll be balls deep in a sexy little redhead." I salute my friends and move away from the bar before I can see them exchanging glances. I know what they think. They think Beck Evans has lost his damn mind. I'm almost inclined to agree with them.

I head up to our room and open the door to find Tease sitting up in bed, hands around her knees. The digital clock on the nightstand says it's later than a whore's bedtime. *We got a day left. One day.* I feel sick to my damn stomach.

She turns to me with a smile and adjusts herself, scooting closer to the edge of the bed. We been fuckin' like rabbits the last few days, but I don't think she's comfortable actually sleeping with me. I wonder if that would change if I just spoke the words aloud, told her the crazy ass thoughts in my head. I don't want her to go – for her sake as well as mine. She loves her club. That much is obvious. But she doesn't like it there, doesn't fit in. It's weird, but somehow, I feel she fits with me.

"I was watching some old western movies," she says, gesturing at the black and white screen. "*Blood on the Moon* is almost over. They're about to start a *Lonesome Dove* marathon." I grin.

"A woman after my own heart. You're telling me you really like to watch these damn things?"

"Who doesn't?" she asks, giving *me* a wink. It ain't often I'm on the receiving end, and I like it. Turns me on. Not that that's surprising. Nobody ever needs to ask Beck Evans if there's a damn banana in his pocket; he's always happy to see 'em. Tease turns back to the screen and sighs, letting her breath out in a slow, controlled motion. I move closer to the bed and pause, looking down at her bare shoulders, the perfect smoothness of her skin. "I'm sorry about earlier," she says, and it takes me a second to figure out what she's talking about. "I shouldn't have brought up the pregnancy thing. I'm not trying to scare you or pressure you into anything. I'm going home on Monday no matter what. There's nothing to worry about."

I sit down hard on the edge of the bed and grab the remote from her, turning off the TV and trying to figure out what to say. I ain't all that good with words.

"The only thing I'm worried about is you. I been lost before, sugar. I know what it's like to be found." She stares at me as I lick my lips and try to figure out if I'm man enough to admit my feelings. This girl is from a rival club, and I don't know how the other Triple M'ers would take it. Still, when I asked her to stay, I meant it. She'd like it here; I'm sure of it. There'd be a price to pay, though. There always is. Melissa. If Tease doesn't go back to her brother, I don't know how I'll get my friend back. I hesitate and the moment passes.

It don't feel good to be stuck between a rock and a hard place.

"I'm gonna grab a real quick shower if you don't mind," I tell Tease and she nods, smiling at me as I stand up and move away. It's hard enough for me to make it to the damn bathroom without looking back, and I can't help but wonder if I got the fuckin' strength to watch her walk away forever.

Tease
CHAPTER 25

Sex.

What does it really mean? How does it define us? I wonder about that as I sit on the edge of the toilet seat with Beck's cell clutched in my hand. I never thought it was that important before, that it was just something you did. At least, that's what I thought on the surface of my mind. Deep down, I must've realized that wasn't true because despite the pressure from the club, I didn't have sex with anyone there. So I guess it always has meant something to me.

Sex with Beck is almost magical in a way. When he touches me, I forget who I am for that period in time, get drawn into him and drown in the experience. It's almost like I *need* him, but does he want me? I can't figure that out. He says stay, but then he doesn't back that up. I don't think I could survive leaving the club if I had to go it alone. I'm used to having the support of others around me all the time.

I want to stand on my own, but I don't think I'm ready for that. My whole life, I've been groomed to be an accessory to others. It's going to take a while to figure this out. If I did join Triple M, and he and I didn't at least experiment and see where this goes, I'd feel lost.

I twist the phone around in my hands.

On the other hand, I'd die for my club. I would. I love everyone there like they're family, an extended sea of brothers and sisters. I just don't feel like that's the right place for me to live my life. I don't want to be anyone's old lady. At least, not anyone in Seventy-seven Brothers. I lean over and put the phone against my forehead. Beck said I could make a quick call to my brother. I'm not sure if he knows exactly what that means or how much last night meant to me.

We watched *Lonesome Dove* side by side on the bed and didn't touch. The absence of it made the sex we've been having all the more interesting. I couldn't stop thinking about it as I fell asleep next to him. When I woke up, our bodies were entangled.

"Shit," I whisper as I dial my brother's number. The longer I sit here, the harder it gets. And there really is no right answer. Beck seems hesitant to say anything more, and I understand. If I don't go back, my brother could flip out. He could kill Beck's friend, Melissa. He might come after Triple M. If I do decide to leave, it can't be right now. Maybe someday. *If Darren even lets you. He barely let go of Lizzie, and he didn't raise her the way he raised you.* I tap my nails against the side of the toilet as I wait for Darren to answer.

"Hello?" he asks, voice tentative. He's not used to getting calls from unknown numbers.

"It's me," I say, and my brother breathes a sigh of relief. "I want to come back today." The words slip from my mouth before I can stop them. *Triple M is going to be pissed.* As for Beck, I think he had some idea of what I was doing. He had to know when I slipped out of bed and asked for his phone. I'm afraid to touch him, to eat another hamburger with him, to walk in the forest. If I do, I might change my mind. *Traitor.* I swallow hard.

"What?" he asks, sounding like he's about ready to blow somebody's head off. "Something happen to you, Tease?" I shake my head emphatically when I realize that he can't see me.

"No. I just … I don't see why we should drag this out any longer." Tax hesitates for an inordinate amount of time before responding. There's something weird in his tone of voice that I don't quite understand.

"Did you arrange this with Triple M?" he asks. God, he knows me too well.

"Yes," I lie, and then because I can't wait any longer, I add, "And did you find Margot?" Darren stays silent for a long moment and then sighs.

"We did. She's under guard at the clubhouse until I figure out what to do with her. Why?" I look up as footsteps approach outside the door and feel my heart start to race. This really is the right thing to do. I have to leave before I get so tangled, I can never undo the knots around my heart.

"Just remember that she's a person and people make mistakes, okay?"

"Mistakes that got our family killed, Tease."

"I know. I'm just telling you to remember that she shouldn't have to suffer. Nobody should." Darren takes a massive breath.

"Are you talking about Margot or something else, Emilie?" I look up at the door, imagining Beck on the other side of it. In my head, he's leaning against it, trying to figure out a way to keep me, desperate for the chance to try. I know it's just a fantasy, but it's an entertaining one.

"I know it's ungodly early, and it's a long drive, but can you make it?"

"I'd ride wherever I had to to get you back, Emilie. You know that." His words make me feel sick to my stomach. I know this isn't the end of the world and that, realistically speaking, I could feasibly meet up with Beck again someday. But it doesn't feel like it.

"This evening then?" I ask him, trying to calculate how long it'll take the club to get here. "Six o'clock?"

"I'll be there, Emilie. I can't wait to see you."

"You, too," I whisper and then there's a click as Darren hangs up. I sit there for a second with a burn in my eyes, tears straining to slide down my face. Life is hard sometimes. Sometimes the price you have to pay is too high, especially if there's a risk involved. This is just one risk I *can't* take. I stand up and open the door, finding Beck leaning against the wall beside it, much like in my fantasy vision. "The trade," I tell him as he grins and starts to stand up. As soon as I say that, his demeanor changes and the smile slides straight off his face. "Today at six."

"The hell you talkin' about?" he asks me, looking baffled and pretty fucking adorable. Beck runs his fingers through his hair as I do my best to avoid looking at his chest. "We were going to go for a ride today, grab another hamburger. You can't do this to me, sugar." He tries to smile again, but I can't smile back. If I do, I'll lose it. I try to keep telling myself that he killed Oren, but it doesn't matter as much as it should. *Family, family, he was family.* I swallow hard.

"I can't do this, Beck. I'm sorry. I'd like to stay, but I can't." I tell him this, watching his facial expression for any sign that I should change my mind. Anything. Instead he just shakes his head and rubs at the stubble on his chin.

"You have to make your own decisions, Emilie," Beck says, but he doesn't elaborate on that thought. Instead he asks me a simple question that both breaks my heart and fractures my soul. "What time are we meetin'?"

CHAPTER 26

I'm standing in a shopping plaza with my heart in my Goddamn throat, my motorcycle parked in a line of others, my club spread out behind me. Opposite us, Seventy-seven Brothers stands somberly. True to our word, Margot walked out of that hotel a free woman and right into the arms of the enemy. So things are peaceful for now. What the hell would happen if I threw up my arms and said fuck it? Grabbed Tease around the waist and dealt with consequences later. It's too damn soon to really understand these fucking feelings I'm having, but I can't stop myself from having them. *Let her go, Beck. It's the best thing for Melissa, the best thing for the club, and the best thing for you. You don't know her. She doesn't know you. This is downright dumb as a dog's butt.*

Tease stands in front of me, facing me, her back to her brother, but she doesn't move.

"Go ahead," I tell her, watching with a tight chest and fists squeezed so tight that blood drips from my palms onto the brick pavers below. "Go on." My voice is gruff and full of pain. I don't know why – ain't like the bitch is being sent off to burn or nothing. Theoretically we could still keep in touch. Theoretically. But we both know it isn't ever going to happen. A long distance relationship? Shoot. I've never even had a close distance relationship. Besides, we might've figured out that our rat fired that first shot, set our clubs at each other's throats, but that doesn't mean Seventy-seven Brothers didn't kill us and ours. Doesn't mean I didn't stab their Sergeant at arms to death. They're good people; we're good people. However, our jackets speak a different language. It'll be a long, long time until we're able to forgive and forget.

Tease starts walking backward, her green eyes on mine, her hand on her chest. In the background, I see Melissa limping forward, face sweaty and eyes far away. But she looks alright, 'specially for somebody that got shot in the damn back. I can look at her later, though. Right now, all I need to see is Tease. I need to memorize the luscious curve of her lips, her perfect nose, her delicately sculpted chin. She sweeps some red hair from her face, her green eyes widening as she continues to move backwards, heels sounding loud on the bricks.

My pulse speeds up so fast, I can hardly keep up, my breath coming in ragged gasps. I almost move after her, but Gaine grabs my shoulder, keeping me back before I do something stupid and spook Seventy-seven Brothers into another firefight. All around us, families laugh, and couples hold hands. The damn plaza is alive and well, and I'm standing here dying inside. I gave myself a weekend to figure my shit out and couldn't manage it. Guess my special Beck bullshit was never meant to be heaped onto one woman.

"Go," I growl out, wishing she'd turn away from me, leave before I have to see the shimmer of tears in her clover green eyes. Tease bites her lip and slows down, still walking backward, still boring into my soul with her gaze. "Go before I say it," I snap at her. I can't be thinkin' this shit. It's so ridiculous. *Do I have that goofy grin on my face*? Not right now, maybe not ever at this rate. But I could. I could and that's why I'm freakin' the fuck out inside.

"Say what, Beck?" she whispers, her voice nearly stolen away in the laughter around us.

"Come on, Tease. It's time to go," her brother says, standing strong and tall by the fountain on the opposite side of the plaza. He's got the same red hair as she does, same green eyes. I can tell from his look of relief that he really does love his sister, but there's something else there. It's not something I could've recognized a few days ago, but it's painfully obvious to me now.

"Shoot," I snarl, moving forward, pulling my arm from Gaine's grasp. As if the universe senses I could use all the help I can get, *Monster You Made* by Pop Evil comes on over the loudspeakers. *Crap.* Now I am for sure done for. As my grandmama would say, *up crap creek with nothin' but your hands for oars.* I walk forward with steady steps, grabbing Tease behind the neck, tangling my fingers in her hair and kissing her mouth with all the heat I got inside of me. All that Beck bullshit. I offer it up on the tip of my tongue, my body vibrating with the weight o' what I just done. *Oh Mother Mary, Beck. You are a stupid fuckin' fool if I ever saw one.*

I pull back from the kiss reluctantly, watching the slight shimmer of tears in Tease's eyes. She's waiting for something from me, something I've never offered up to another woman in this life. I been savin' it. Used to think that was because I never wanted to fall in love. Now I know it's because I hadn't ever found someone I wanted to fall in love with. If I feel this strongly after a couple of days, how will I feel in a couple of years? How's this for an answer: I don't give a shit. Live in the motherfuckin' moment, baby.

"What did you want to say?" she whispers, her voice barely audible over the sound of the music swirling in notes and colors all around me. I raise my chin and my voice, just so everybody can hear, so they can know how damn serious I am.

I slip my jacket off my shoulders and take a deep breath.

"Emilie 'Tease' Hathorne … " I say, holding it out to her, offering myself up in leather and patches and honest to God truth and humility. I get caught on the words, but just for a second, when she starts to turn away. Tease pounds across the pavement while I stand there with my heart hanging out of my chest and my life bleedin' away, leaving me dry and desperate. "Emilie!" I shout, dropping my jacket to my side, ready to run after her. "I love you, Goddamn it. I didn't want to, but I do. I really fuckin' do."

She spins to face me, red hair billowing out around her face. The tears she was holding back finally fall, sliding down her cheeks. I wait for her to come to me, prayin' that she will, hopin' to God that nobody makes fun of me for this. I'd hate to have to bust some faces. She smiles at me with that beautiful half-smile and then turns to her brother, throwing her arms around him and giving him a massive hug that I can't help but be jealous of. Her property patches stare me in the face, mocking me, making me sick to my Goddamn stomach. I almost stomp over there and tear her from his arms, but what good would that do for me? She has to come willingly or it don't mean shit.

The song begins to wind down, and I start to turn away when I see her stepping back and sliding her arms out of the jacket. Tease touches her fingers to the fabric and looks up at her brother.

"I love you, Tax," she says and he smiles sadly, pursing his lips a bit.

"I know. And I love you, too, Tease."

"This isn't goodbye forever, just for now." She hands him her jacket and he takes it gingerly, letting it hang over his arm as she moves backward again, spinning around and taking off across the pavement in a run. I don't move, too scared to even dream that this means what I think it means.

Tease throws herself into my arms, wrapping her hands around my neck and kissing me again, letting words tumble from her lips that only I can hear. "I love you, too, Beck. I'm not a hundred percent certain what that means yet, but I'm willing to take a chance and find out. I've never risked anything in my life, but here, now, I have to. This feels right."

The song comes to an end, leaving an empty space of silence in the busy sunshine of the day. I look over Tease's shoulder and meet Tax's eyes.

"You going to let us ride out of here with your sister?" I ask as Melissa pauses near us. I switch my gaze to her blue eyes, smiling big as I can. She knows I won't leave her here either. I'll fight to the death for these women if I have to.

"It was supposed to be an even trade," Tax says, and my body stiffens. I got my .38 in my pants, so if I have to, I can blow his Goddamn head off. But I don't want to. I don't want our new beginning bathed in blood. "A girl for a girl. You're keeping mine, so ... " I watch that expression come back over Tax's face, watch as he walks forward and pauses next to Melissa. *Hah, I fucking knew it! Triple M is cursed. Cursed, I tell ya. We got the fever and it seems to be spreading. Love. Fuck. What a disease.* They stare into one another's eyes for a moment before Mel glances over at me and winks hard, that sultry smile tilting up her lips. *Uh oh.* I hope this man knows that Diamond isn't just any ol' lady. She'll give him a run for his fucking money. Tax opens up Tease's jacket and waits with a questioning look on his face.

A moment later, Mel lets him help her gingerly into it.

Beck
Epilogue

After I said goodbye to Mel, kissing her cheek and wishin' with all my heart for her to find a happy ending, we walk back to our bikes and pause there for a moment in silence. All around me, Triple M'ers stand in quiet contemplation.

"I hope y'all are okay with this?" I ask, looking around the group. Austin steps up beside me and scans his eyes over the remaining forty members of our little group of outcasts, misfits, and fuck-ups. I make sure to catch Gaine, Mireya, and Kimmi's gazes. But they're all smiling at me. Of course they are. Friends till the bitter fuckin' end, right?

"Because if you're not, then walk away now. Today, we start a new chapter of Triple M." Austin holds up his hand. "Motorcycles, madness, money. We ride the first, own the second, and figure out a way to survive on the third. I know it hasn't been easy since Kent's been gone, but I promise from this day forward, it'll get better. Life always gets better." Austin glances over at Amy, and for once in my life, I'm happy I caught this particular disease. Love. Who'da thunk, huh? "Those of you that are with us, remember that we have to have each other's backs. We have to trust explicitly, love indiscriminately, and live like today's the last sunset we'll ever see." Austin leans over and presses a kiss to Amy's pink lips. "Now hop on your fuckin' bikes and let's get the hell out of here."

I grin and pull Tease against me, kissing her mouth with all the worry I had inside of me, all the fear that she wouldn't come back across that plaza and take me up on my crazy ass offer.

"Falling in love in a few days is stupid as shit," I tell her, and she raises an eyebrow. "But I'm stupid as shit, crazy, too. So I think it works." I give her a big grin and watch as she smiles back.

"Life is crazy as shit. I think we're right on track." Tease pulls away from me and climbs on my bike, her small body the perfect size for the little Suzuki. *Might be time for me to get a new ride soon.* I crawl up behind her, sliding my arms on either side of her perfect body.

"Amen to that, sugar tits," I tell her, kissing her ear and starting up my ride. One last glance over my shoulder shows me Melissa and Tax making out on the back of his chopper. I grin and kick off, following after Austin until we get where we're going. I don't expect it, not at first, but as we get closer, my smile grows wider. *Hot damn. Hot fucking damn.*

When our bikes pull up outside the dilapidated house, the one with the three car garage, Scar Tissue starts playing on the intercom system. A collective groan ripples through the group, half irritation, half relief. Wholly satisfied.

"You asked for a clubhouse," Austin says as he takes off his helmet, waiting for the rest of us to follow suit. There's a nervous look on his face, but he's a smart man, I think he'll get over it. "Well, here it is."

"Here it fuckin' is," I say, pulling my helmet off and resting my chin on Tease's head, smelling her hair, absorbing her scent. This is going to take a while to get used to, but I think that one day, Seventy-seven Brothers might have a run for its money in Triple M. I tighten my arms around Tease and hold her as close as I can. "Home sweet fucking home."

And I'm not just talking about the damn house.

*Austin and Amy are back in book four of the Triple M 'MC'
Series. Releases May 25th, 2014.*

AMAZON BESTSELLING AUTHOR
C.M. STUNICH

Real Ugly(Hard Rock Roots #1)

Excerpt Included!

CHAPTER 1

❧ NAOMI KNOX ❧

There's a metamorphosis happening right before my eyes. I'm watching a devil shed its skin, shrink its horns and grow wings. The dark haze in the air is lifting, banished by the bright lights of the stage. Even metaphorically, a trick like that is hard to pull off. I'm impressed. Or I would be if I didn't hate the asshole so much.

"He looks like a fucking angel," I whisper as I sip my beer.

"What?" Blair shouts, cupping her hand around my ear. I swipe some hair away from my face and lean over, so that she can hear me above the booming of the bass. It pounds down through the wood of the stage, into the concrete, and across the floor where it catches on the rubber soles of my boots and ricochets up through my bones. If I close my eyes, I can see it tainting my blood, forcing my heart to pump faster and faster, until I feel dizzy from the beautiful poison in the air. The phrase *slaying the crowd* wasn't made

1

up off the top of someone's head; if the fucks on stage do it right, it really does feel like the music is killing you softly.

"Turner Campbell," I yell back at her, my lips brushing against the small, black plugs in her earlobes. "He looks like a fucking angel up there." Blair leans back and raises one pierced brow at me. Her blue eyes say that I'm full of shit. I take another sip of cool, cool amber and watch as she turns her heart shaped face to the stage. Her gaze rakes Turner from head to toe and then slides across the heaving, thumping crowd, landing right back on me.

"A fallen angel," she shouts. Pauses. "*Maybe.*"

I shrug and ignore her pointed stare, watching Turner as he moves across the stage, lights glistening off the blue-black highlights in his hair and making him look like he has a damn halo on his head. His brown eyes scan the crowd, catching on faces and holding them as he purrs into the microphone and caresses it like he fucking *owns* it. I bet every bitch in here can practically feel his hands on her body, taste his tongue in her mouth. *What am I shitting myself for? They've probably all had a nice, big slice of the real thing anyway.* Let's just say that Turner's reputation proceeds him.

Devil.

I have to remember that he's not just a devil, but *The Devil.*

I take another sip of beer and try to focus on something else – the crowd of people clusterfucking at the bar, the mosh pit up front, Blair's white feather eyelashes. Nothing works. My gaze finds Turner Campbell again and stays there, focusing primarily on his lips and the words that tumble out of them.

"*What the hell did you do to leave me broken, barren, and bleeding? What gave you the fucking right?*" Turner sucks in a massive lungful of air, blowing his hot breath across the microphone and breaking my heart with a single gasp. I'm not alone. The crowd starts to hum, men and women alike pulsing with the heat and the energy of the song. *Goddamn, that's good,* I think as I allow myself to sink against the cool concrete of the back wall. *Doubt those lyrics are his though. Fucking hypocrite.* Just yesterday I walked in on Turner fucking a roadie over a PA speaker. When he saw me, he just pulled out and left the girl there with her panties around her ankles. She cried for a half a fucking hour. *Devil.* I want to hate him, but it's really hard from down here. I like it better when I'm backstage, when I can look at him hitting on groupies and roadies, watch him running his fingers across the lips of a dozen girls in a dozen cities. It's a lot easier to hate him that way. *How am I going to make it through six months of this?*

I finish my beer and push away from the wall, dropping the empty bottle on the edge of the bar before sneaking out a side door. My hands slide across a collage of torn stickers and scribbled Sharpie as I heave the heavy metal out of my way, snatching one last glance before I go at the lead singer of Indecency. Sweat slides down the tattoos on his neck and soaks into the fabric of his black T-shirt. Ironically, it's one of ours. *Amatory Riot.* I doubt he even really knows who we are. I bet one his roadie bitches dressed him this morning.

I drop the door shut behind me, not caring that the sound of it slamming is like a gunshot in the still air outside the Pound. I'm glad our set is over because it would be hard to follow an act like that. No matter what I think of Turner, his band is good. I guess they'd have to be since they're the headliners. Still …

I put a cigarette between my lips and light up. The tangy coastal air feels good against my moist skin and the breeze smells like salt, waking me from the buzzed trance I was nursing and thrusting me back into the real world. Not always a good thing.

"Hey, Naomi," a voice calls out from the end of the alley. I don't turn my head because there's only one person I've ever met that sounds like a demonic version of Mickey Mouse. "Hayden got drunk and vomited all over the bathroom. There's like three inches of fucking puke in there." Wren pauses next to me and tucks his skinny hands into the front pockets of his acid washed jeans. "It smells like tequila and it's making me sick." I take a drag on my cigarette and close my eyes. The music from inside is drifting through the walls and poking the bare skin on my arms like a chorus of needles. I sigh and flick my smoke to the grimy cement.

"So clean it up," I tell him as I crush the butt to ashes with the toe of my stiletto boot. "I'm tired of being Hayden's bitch." Wren watches me, but doesn't say anything else. He knows I'll do it. That I'll walk in there and pick our lead singer up off the floor, wipe her down and strip her naked, put her to bed and tell her a goddamn fairy tale. I'm no stranger to cleaning up Hayden's messes. I just have to get my head in the right place before I do it. Wren shifts his weight to the side and continues to stare. "Fuck, don't just stand there and stare at me. You know I'll friggin' do it. Gimme a minute, why don't you?"

I turn away and start down the alley, back towards the front where bouncers in black shirts wait, passing around a silver flask and sharing a joint. They know me, so they don't say anything, just watch as I step into their circle and reach out my hand. Both items make their way to me quickly.

"I love your shit, Knox," says a man with bright blue eyes and a tattoo of a dragon curling up his left arm. I swig some of the alcohol from the flask. *Ugh. Cheap whiskey.* I wipe my hand across my mouth and hand it the person standing next to me.

"My shit?" I ask as I pinch the joint between my fingers and slide it into my mouth. I take a nice, long drag and wait for the smoke to fill my lungs and cloud my brain. I can't look at Hayden if I don't get fucked up first. Ever since that day, the sight of her makes me sick to my stomach. *God, I hate that bitch.*

"Your music. It's good shit." I blow white smoke into the air and smile with tight lips.

"If you ever call my music *shit* again," I say as I pass the joint to dragon-boy. "I will kick your fucking ass to the curb."

I make out with dragon-boy for awhile and stop just short of second base. He seems pretty pissed off, but I'm not a fucking whore, and I'm just not that into sex right now. My head feels light and fluffy, like it's been stuffed with cotton, and I'm having trouble walking. I have to stop in the alley and sit on the dirty cement, so I can take my stilettos off. It isn't easy to navigate in four inch heels, especially with the alcohol and the THC roiling around inside of me.

I throw the leather boots over my arm and stumble back to the bus, fully expecting to find Hayden right where Wren left her – drunk and drowning in puke. When I open the door, I get a whole other story.

"Right there, baby," Hayden is growling, hands curled around the edge of the countertop. Behind her, Turner Campbell is thrusting his dick like he's in a fucking marathon or something, gripping her skinny hips with white knuckles and squeezing his eyes shut tight. He doesn't even look up when I ascend the creaky steps.

"What the fuck, Hayden?" I ask, but she's so out of it that she doesn't hear me. Turner does, I can tell, but he doesn't respond either. Doesn't stop. The wet sound of their bodies sliding together makes my stomach twist dangerously. Vomit climbs my throat, but I swallow it back. "Hey, motherfucker," I snarl, forgetting instantly about that angelic presence I saw on stage. It was all a trick of the light, a nice, fat slice of show business that he shoved down everybody's throat – including mine. He's back to being a devil again. How could I have ever forgotten? After what he did to me before, I should slit his freaking throat and toss him out the window, let the stray dogs in the alley finish him off. "Get off of her! She's fucking wasted, you asshole." I throw my boots on the floor and move forward, putting one hand on Turner's chest and shoving him back. He stumbles and hits the cabinets with a grunt, sliding to the floor with his dick hanging out of his pants and his shirt bunched up around his midsection. Bits of spiderweb peek out at me from under the black fabric of his tee, crawling down and wrapping his cock. He's even got tattoos on the damn thing. You'd think I'd have noticed that before, but I guess I was too busy getting my cherry popped to think about much else.

"What the hell?" he moans, putting a hand to his head and rubbing at his forehead with fingers wrapped in ink. When Turner pushes his hair back, the edges of star tattoos wink at me from his hairline. He's obviously trashed as shit, too, and doesn't make even a halfhearted attempt to stand up on his own. I roll my eyes and ignore him, throwing an arm around Hayden's waist as she tilts to the side and threatens to topple over. I don't have much love for the bitch, but if she dies, Amatory Riot is pretty much screwed sideways. It would be a sort of love/hate thing for me if she were to fall and crack her head open.

"Goddamn it, Lee," I growl at her as I drag her boney ass across the floor and kick open the doors to the sleeper section of the bus. Hayden is still covered in puke, so I force her to stumble into the shower and let her slump the floor. I turn the water on *cold.*

"Shit!" she shouts, her voice trailing off into a moan. Hayden's head slams into the tile wall and she starts to sob. "What are you doing to me?" she cries as I step back and run a hand through my hair. Blair is glancing at me from her position on the floor of the second bathroom, a sponge in one hand and a bucket in the other. Looks like most of the vomit is gone.

"Thanks," I say, but she's already shaking her head, tossing the sponge into the bucket and sitting up. The knees of her jeans are soaked through and her white tee is stained with something questionable. She looks pissed.

"Don't thank me, Naomi," she says as she stands up and leans against the door frame, popping a cig in her mouth as she relaxes against the wood. "This is Hayden's oversight, Hayden's tequila, Hayden's mess." Blair takes a drag and throws the cigarette into the bucket. "Stop taking responsibility for her shit." I don't respond because Blair doesn't know what happened between Hayden and me. If she did, she'd understand. I don't like her thinking I'm Hayden's lapdog, but what can I do about it? The bitch has shit on me for days. *God, I am so super fucked.* I shrug and turn around, ignoring the grunts of irritation from the bunk on my right.

"Fuck you, Wren," I snarl as I move past him and take note of the other bunk. *Looks like Kash is in tonight. What a surprise.* Kash is having some kind of fucked up affair with two chicks – the driver for Indecency and the bassist from Terre Haute. He almost never spends the night on our bus.

I pause in the doorway and stare down at Turner Campbell and his flaccid dick.

"Get up, Turner," I bark at him, moving forward and poking his leg with my toes. "And get the fuck out. Go." He moans, but he doesn't move. I think he's even drooling on his shoulder. *Pathetic. If your groupies could only see you now.* "Turner. Get the hell off of my bus."

"What is your problem?" he whispers, sharp lips barely moving with the words. He sounds lucid enough, but he looks like shit. I put my hands on my hips and try to make a judgment call. It isn't easy with my head swimming like the Northern Pacific. I could go and grab one of Turner's band members, see if they'd come and get him, but I dread going on that bus in the middle of the night. That is, if their stupid ass bodyguard will even let me pass. Besides, the odds of finding anybody in that band that isn't trashed at this hour are pretty slim.

"Stand up," I command as I watch his hand travel between his legs, snap the empty condom off and toss it onto our carpet. My lips curl into a sneer, and I end up grabbing his arm and dragging him up off the floor. His skin is hot to the touch and sweaty as hell. *Please don't OD on my bus, you stupid fuck,* I think as I struggle to pull the world's biggest asshole to his feet. I don't like the man, by any means, but if he dies then I'm guessing they'll probably cancel the rest of the tour, and that would be a big ass, fucking drag for me and my band. Guess the least I can do is prevent him from drowning in his own vomit tonight. If keeping him on his back and wiping dribble from his chin will keep my dream afloat then the rest of the world be damned, I'll fucking do it. I can always take pictures as backup and sell them to the tabloids if everything goes to hell.

"Shit, Naomi," he growls, and I drop his arm like it's poisoned. Turner falls to his knees in front of me and leans against the wall, head hanging down between my legs and hands flat on the floor. "Just leave me alone. Leave me the fuck alone."

I stare down at the back of his neck, at the inky paw prints that climb his spine and disappear into his dark hair.

"What did you just say?"

Turner groans and lets himself slump fully against the cabinet before he opens his mouth and vomits right past that beautiful, little tongue ring of his. *What a friggin' douche,* I think, and then before I can stop it, my brain adds, *that remembers your name.* Hearing the three syllables of my earthly monicker pass through his lips was nothing short of a shot to the back of the head. I didn't even think that he knew the name of my band, let alone mine personally.

"Ah, shit," Blair says from behind me, making me jump as she sidles around me and stares down at the growing stain on the carpet. "This is great. Just great. Now we get to drive all the way to San Diego with the smell of Turner Campbell's puke." She smiles at me with tight lips. "But hey, what's new, right? I feel like we're eternally in this fucker's shadow." She kicks Turner with the pointed toe of her red heel. "Still think he looks like an angel?"

I sigh.

"Just shut up, Blair, and help me pick him up."

She frowns at me and tucks some of her blonde and black hair behind an ear while I dig my arms under Turner's pits and try to drag him to his feet.

"And what, pray tell, are we going to do with him once we get him up?" she asks as she bends down and joins me, tits practically spilling out the top of the tight corset she's got on. All three of us groan as we shift Turner's comatose body between us, leaving his legs dangling on the ground like perverted puppet masters in the world's worst marionette show.

"Just put him in my bed," I say as I ignore another pointed stare from Blair.

"He's totally out, Mi. I doubt he could even get it up right now."

"Blair, seriously?" I ask her as we dump him on the bottom bunk and shove his legs up onto my black comforter. "I'm not even going to respond to that," I tell her as I hear a whimper from the bathroom and suddenly remember that I've left Hayden in an ice old shower. *Oops.* Blair and I exchange a look, and she sighs.

"Yes, I will clean up Campbell's puke as long as you don't start apologizing for him, too."

"Fuck him," I say.

"Good girl," she tells me and spins away on her heel while I retreat back to the bathroom and switch off the water. Hayden is curled into a fetal position, sobbing, and while that's not unusual, it's kind of disturbing to watch.

I grab a towel from under the sink and throw it to her. It hits her in the face and falls to the floor. Hayden lets out a wail that makes my teeth hurt, and I suddenly regret grabbing the bitch before she fell. *Should've let her crack her head wide open,* I think as I step forward and start to strip her down. She doesn't protest, just flops around limply and lets me tear off her expensive, designer clothing that's supposed to scream 'I'm a rebel!', but instead just makes her look like a fucking tool.

"Come on," I say to her as I grab her by the wrists. Don't need any help lifting this bitch. She weighs, like, maybe eighty freaking pounds. "You stupid, anorexic, motherfucker," I snort as I drag Hayden into the hallway and practically shove her onto the bunk opposite Turner. As soon as her wet head hits the pillow, she starts to snore. I watch her for a moment and turn away, catching a glimpse of Turner's shuttered eyelids and gently parted lips. Believe it or not, he looks like a fucking angel again. I flick one of his lip piercings with my fingernails and move back into the kitchen/living room area with a sigh. The pot and the whiskey have already abandoned me and left me alone with nothing but stark, white reality. "Is it wrong to hate someone so much it hurts?" I ask Blair as she sprays the rug with some sort of organic cleaner that I just know isn't going to work. The last one she used was made out of tropical fruit and smelled like bubble gum; the piss stain on the hallway floor is still there. Enough said.

"Are you talking about Hayden or Turner?" Blair asks as

we both look up and watch our driver/roadie/personal bitch, Spencer Harmon, step into the RV. She's got two armfuls of groceries and a wrinkled lip.

"God, what is that smell?" she asks as she sets the bags down and watches Blair go back to work, leather clad ass up in the air flashing a three inch line of butt crack. If I was into chicks, it'd be kind of hot.

"Turner Campbell's leftovers," I say as I pop in a cigarette and smoke it with short, sharp puffs like it's a cigar or some shit. I watch with disgust as goose bumps spring up all over Spencer's arms and legs. Her full lips part gently and her dark lashes flutter.

"Turner Campbell was here?" she whispers, and I can't hold back the scowl that crosses my face. I shouldn't get so annoyed at the girl. I mean, she's only one of thousands who've fallen for that man's charisma. *Myself included.*

"Yeah, and he's trashed as shit. I walked in on him and Hayden fucking."

"Hey," Blair snaps as she sits up and pushes her bucket away, wiping an arm across her forehead. "I had to watch the whole thing happen and even *listen* to it." I ignore her, and I don't ask why she didn't put a stop to it. Nobody stands up to Hayden except for me, and even then, it's questionable. Same thing goes for Turner Campbell, but not because he's scary like Hayden. He's just a god of the stage. He can do no wrong. I resist the urge to spit on the floor. It's already bad enough down there.

"Oh," Spencer says, but the wonder in her brown eyes doesn't die and her skin prickles and crackles like it's been lit on fire. She removes the groceries like she's in a daze, pulling out healthy snacks like celery and carrots and broccoli that only she and Blair will eat. I can only hope there's something in there that's loaded up with carbs and sugar. "What time did he leave?"

"He didn't," I say, gesturing over my shoulder with my chin. I stab my cigarette out in an ashtray that's overflowing onto the table and shrug nonchalantly. "He's so fucked up that he couldn't stand. I put him in my bed." Spencer's eyes open wide, and I have to cut her off before she can even offer. "No, I'll sleep on the couch," I say and I can practically see her heart bursting out of her chest at the thought of spending the night within touching distance of Mr. Campbell. As irritating as the whole scene is, I'm glad because there is no way in shit that I would spend another night anywhere near that man. The first was bad enough. *Jesus, Naomi, that was six years ago. Get the fuck over it. You know he doesn't remember, so why should you?*

"Look at you," Blair says as she stands up, pulling the bucket along with her. "All empathetic and shit. Good for you, Naomi."

"Fuck you," I say as I give her the finger, grab a can of beer from the fridge and curl up on the black sofa that sits across from the door. I pop the top and nurse my drink while I watch Spencer finish putting away the groceries. When she's done, she just stands there and wrings her hands like she's about to walk into an interview or something. "He doesn't bite," I say and immediately wish I hadn't. *Oh, wait. Yes, yes, he does.* I suck down half my can as I watch her watching me.

"You really do hate him, don't you?" she asks, and I shrug nonchalantly. But when I speak, I'm dead fucking serious. I raise my eyes to meet Spencer's.

"More than anyone else on this godforsaken earth."

About the Author

C.M. Stunich was raised under a cover of fog in the area known simply as Eureka, CA. A mysterious place, this strange, arboreal land nursed Caitlin's (yes, that's her name!) desire to write strange fiction novels about wicked monsters, magical trains, and Nemean Lions (Google it!). She currently enjoys drag queens, having too many cats, and tribal bellydance.

She can be reached at author@cmstunich.com, and loves to hear from her readers. Ms. Stunich also wrote this biography and has no idea why she decided to refer to herself in the third person.

Happy reading and carpe diem!

www.cmstunich.com

Printed in Great Britain
by Amazon